IRISH TOWN

MATTHEW JOHN MEAGHER

A NOVEL

PRAISE FOR IRISH TOWN

"Mixing the best parts of *The Spectacular Now* and *The Hunger Games*, Matt weaves a captivating tale of love, loss and teenage boy angst. Few books seem to be written for the normal, hormone-driven teenage boy, and Matt does a great job of channeling the thoughts of a young man coming into his own as he falls head over heels for a girl who he also must recruit for a dangerous mission that might almost certainly kill her."

—**Traci Jones, winner of the Coretta Scott King/Steptoe New Talent Award and author of *Silhouetted by the Blue, Standing Against the Wind,* and *Finding My Place***

"… powerfully reminiscent of *Lord of the Flies* and *A Clockwork Orange.*"

—**Mario Acevedo, author of *Felix Gomez* vampire novels**

"Matt Meagher has written a ticking emotional time bomb, and you won't be able to put it down until it explodes."

—**David Hicks author of *White Plains***

"Equal parts *A Clockwork Orange* and *Harry Potter, Irish Town* is a gripping teenage coming-of-age story about students coming together, navigating the dystopian (and sometimes deadly) politics of their rival towns."

—**Jason Masino, writer**

"*Irish Town* is a story full of twists and turns. I found myself unable to put it down!"

—**Mike Carletta**

"There are two distinct landscapes in *Irish Town.* The first is the external landscape that Matt creates, a dystopia that reflects real world problems including climate change, substance abuse and issues of class. The second landscape is the internal one of his main character, a teenage boy named Jeremiah Connelly, nicknamed Jester, through whom the story is narrated. Jester is too clever for his own good, at times crass, cocky and incurably horny; but he's also fiercely loyal to his friends and maintains a sort of youthful innocence. In this way, Matt has created a character very likely to resonate with his readers."

—**Ally Levise, writer**

IRISH TOWN

MATTHEW JOHN MEAGHER

A NOVEL

Independently Published under the auspices of MARSMEN Ltd.
www.matthewjmeagher.com

First published in the United States in 2020

Epigraph credit: excerpted "The Things They Carried." by Tim O'Brien, © Tim O'Brien, Houghton Mifflin Harcourt, 1990.

Names: Meagher, Matthew John, author
Title: Irish Town
Subjects: Young adult fiction | Social Themes | Friendship | Drug, alcohol, and substance abuse

Typeset by Zvonimir Bulaja, Booknook.biz
Cover illustration by Kateri Kramer
Interior Art by Kateri Kramer

To find out more about the author, visit www.matthewjmeagher.com

This novel is dedicated to my mother,
Sharon Meagher.
These characters would not live without you.

"… story-truth is truer sometimes than happening-truth."

—Tim O'Brien

"Love's never died; it just looks a little different these days."

—Irish Slay

CONTENTS

PART I.

THE HALL

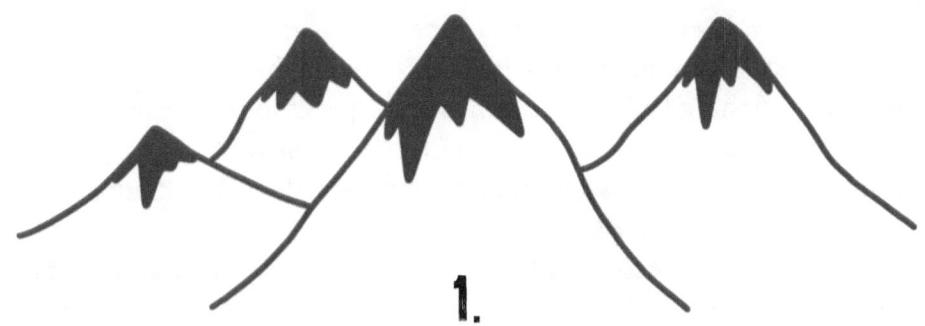

1.

JESTER

POWDER MATCH: 60 DAYS

I TAKE A SHOT OF cheap whiskey. The sun creeps an orange hue through my window. I take another shot to get me to normal and begin my school day. My name is Jeremiah Connelly. Most people call me Jester.

In the reflection of a cracked and scratched mirror, I see a woman creeping through my neighbor's backyard wearing only a parka and snow boots, carrying her black high heels. I hear a sliding door open. I crouch down and peek over my window sill. As she escapes, I see my neighbor with another woman. It's his teenage daughter.

My neighbor is huge and jacked. His muscles ripple across his shoulders as he breathes. He's sprawled out on the bed naked with one leg hanging over the side.

His daughter whips the other woman's G-string panties off his lampshade, holds them between her two fingers like a biohazard, and throws them in the hamper. She turns on the shower, tiptoes over to the bed, grabs empty beer cans and an ashtray to dump into the trash. She slaps the back of his thinning grey hair to wake him. He continues to lie motionless. She slaps his back and he wakes up. She hands him a cup of coffee and turns to open his closet to pick out his outfit for the day.

He gulps down the coffee and tops it off with a shot from a flask. With one eye open, he trudges his way to the bathroom, and sees that she has everything laid out for him: a shirt, pre-knotted tie, pants, belt, socks, and shoes. When he comes out, she cleans up his spotty beard with a razor and styles his hair. He actually looks like a functioning adult.

At least she has a dad.

I look at my reflection in the mirror. A crack in the glass stretches over a scar that reaches from my right brow to my chin. Cherries broke it in last year's Powder Match. The scar is the only masculine thing I have. I suffer from resting baby face. I'm a high schooler who looks thirteen. With my hood up, I look bald. I drag myself over to a closet filled with black hoodies, all saying "Jester" on the back. One good thing about being the Jester is my hoodies. They're impermeable. Since it's cold year-round up here now, keeping warm is something I don't have to worry about. I jump when I hear Mom's voice boom, "Jester! Irish is here!" I turn to get a last look at my neighbor through my window. He's sitting and staring right at me.

He looks familiar.

I pull my hood up over my head, run downstairs and out the door, grabbing my scarf as I go. I follow my adorable demon dog—Dooby. She's an oversized wiener dog with the fury of a Pitbull. She doesn't lick my toes; she *bites* them.

A steel-black limo pulls up to the front door. Old brakes screech as the limo that I fixed up over the summer arrives. There is still a rusted steel door on the rear passenger side, but that's nothing compared to the battered "tin can" Irish had presented me back in June. He's a kid that can get things.

The icy, snowy wind makes it hard to see, but I can follow Dooby waddling to the limo door. I wrap the white scarf around my neck and pull the hoodie strings tight. A plume of smoke billows out as the door opens. As I enter the limo, I join Ashton's Irish Brigade, a nickname the town has given us. The limo reeks of a decade ago when we were children. Cracked leather, old whiskey, stale smoke, and windows black as holes; it's like riding in a vintage hearse. In the middle of the limo is a blinking three-dimensional tele-screen showing the weather. Big surprise... it's gonna be cold and windy.

Dooby jumps on Curly's lap. Curly Brown is our Smoke Quartermate. Smoke Quartermates raise Demon Dogs and deal drugs. Tall, pale, and skinny, his long, dreaded hair is folded into a bun making his hoodie look like a helmet. He, Dooby, and Irish are sitting across from me.

Irish sits with his brother, Twitch. They cradle fresh bundles of wood and chug bottles of water. Irish always has water. I don't know how he gets it since the Cherries control the Dam. He who has water, has power. The mountain wetlands have dried up and the western slope is in a never-ending drought. It snows in the winter, but barely enough to cover the valley. Snowdrop Resort is one of the only remaining mountain resorts in the country. The drought forces the Cherries to make their own snow.

Irish doesn't drink, but he smokes like a chimney. His eyes are cold and black. His flush skin is rugged and life-ridden. His massive frame barely fits in the limo, and his hoodie pulls tight over his broad shoulders. A tattooed clover, in tribute to his mom, drips from his left eye, and a thick Celtic cross wrapped in a rose covers his neck. His sharp jaw-line and thick beard give the image of a full-grown man. Girls swoon every time he enters a room, but he doesn't give them a chance. Irish couldn't fight in last year's Powder Match. He was in the hospital. His dad had beaten the hell out of him. Twitch replaced him and the Cherries beat him to a pulp. He's a different person now. Irish takes him to school and makes sure he has water and food. Other than that, Twitch just stays in his room working on his art.

Shea Murdoch sits up front with our driver, Freshmore Quartermate Benny. Shea is smaller than Irish, but has the dense, compact aspect of a bowling ball. His smoky-grey eyes and buzzed brown hair show a "back off" vibe. He cracks his knuckles as a toothpick hangs from his lips. Shea is part of the Brigade, but not a Quartermate. His family has been in Ashton since the mining days. He knows the ins and outs of the valley.

Quartermates are leaders in the community appointed by Irish. Benny, our driver, leads the Freshman and Sophomores.

I say, "What up, fellas? We gonna do something different this year? Elect some smart kids? Give me some help in Academia? Or are we still going with a bunch of candy asses for the Snow Brawl?"

5

Shea nods towards Irish.

Irish says, "There's my Jester. Cynical and drunk. Lucky you're smart."

"Get off your cross, Irish," I say. He turns away and stares out the window as I place two cubes of ice into a glass and shower it with spiced rum.

He says, "We do what Vivian wants."

We leave my neighborhood, Ashton Hills. A few families live up here, but most houses are deserted. We turn the corner past a rusted Bachelor Loop sign. The Loop is a gravel road tourists use to explore some old ghost towns. We don't want Ashton to become a ghost town. Powder Valley is hidden miles west in the Rocky Mountains. Sometimes we get hikers who brave the trek, but the "Falling Rock" or "Watch Out for Bears" signs deter people from getting too close.

Irish speaks with a hoarse tone as he plays with the flame of his lighter. He sniffs the air, coughs, and says, "Must be Monday. Smells like cinnamon."

The Sugar Sweet factory bubbles brown cinnamon smoke. The factory has a history. It was once the home of an Irish silver mining operation, but the mine went dry and the owner was forced to figure out a way to employ Ashton with a factory with no material to make product. Horatio Steele's family owned the plant then. A hundred years ago, his great grandson, Trenton, converted the facility into a candy factory, using old family recipes for various kinds of sweets. Now his son Bart runs the Sugar Sweet Factory and employs nearly the entire town. When the opioid crisis hit, Bart's concoctions became medicinal. They can heal or enhance, sometimes even cure diseases. We make the Sweets. We don't consume them. Cherries do. The Cherries use special Sweet concoctions to beat us in the Powder Match by getting stronger and healing faster. Sweets we sure as hell can't afford. So the smell is a slap in the face every Monday morning.

Curly sits, rolling a joint in a flame with his long bony fingers. He reaches from his left ear and asks, "j for me J.?"

"Nah… I'm good," I say.

He takes a cig stick from his right ear, places it in my mouth, and lights it.

"Thanks, Curly. You know I hate the first day of school."

6

"All good, bruh. Where's Mars at?" Curly asks. Mars is our Five-Points Quartermate. Five-Points is a project community in town.

Benny interjects: "Neveah's coming in this year as a freshman. She's trying to pass my Quarter straight to Mars's."

Neveah is Mars's younger sister. I have to be careful when talking about her around Mars. Everyone does. She's ridiculously good-looking. He sent a few of his Quarterminions to mash a kid who gave her a Valentine… in the third grade. I saw her running laps on the track the other day, and I swear the girl looked like she belonged in college.

Benny pushes a dash-app that links to a town website and puts on Dropkick Murphy's, an old Irish band, broadcasting their songs on the internet to let the town know we're heading through.

We pass the squalor of Ashton. Men and women stumble across icy sidewalks and rats scurry from beneath their feet. Other rats dig through the pockets of the passed-out drunks that litter trash-strewn streets like discarded bottles. Broken windows gaze from crumbling buildings. A pall of smoke hangs over everything. Ashton is similar to the ruins of winter war-torn ghettos. Each building, burnt grey, cracked and broken, resembles an old Depression photograph.

Ashtonians have always been fighters. They fought in all the wars. Ashton is known for its soldiers. PTSD is as much part of the town as is the dirty air.

We stop at a back entrance to the Sugarsweet Factory. Irish, using one palm, hands Curly a few racks of bottled water, and in less than a minute, Curly makes the exchange. He jumps back in the limo with a bag full of Sweets. Sweets may not be physically addicting, but they feel like heaven. Some of the concoctions have been known to cure dementia. But the hell we live in, anything good is hard to come by. Ashtonians use the Sweets to fill their opioid addictions.

I pour myself another drink. Minutes pass in silence as we drive down the mountain from the factory into Five-Points. We stop at the food kitchen. Half the town lines up around the corner. Irish knocks on the inside window for Benny to stop. Benny rolls the window down and one of Mars's minions reaches in for the bundles of wood and Sweets. People huddle and jump on the kid. Benny pushes the gas and we drive to school.

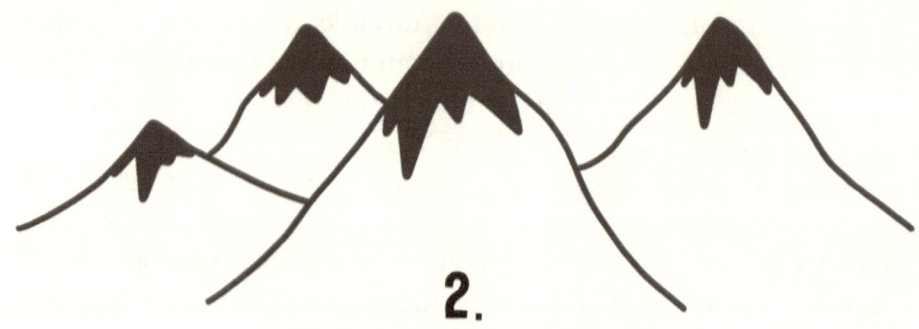

2.

ASHTON HIGH

I DON'T KNOW WHAT'S worse, a hangover or Ashton High. Approaching Ashton High makes me hold down vomit. The pride of the town is cemented in towering maroon brick with skinny vertical windows. It's similar to a prison. Kids rush inside from the cold. We pull off to the east side of the school and drop off Twitch. He's a Nerd like me. Even though I know I'm going to see him in a few minutes, I feel I've lost a friend for life every time he leaves.

Damn, Cherries.

We drive to the west side of school and park next to the fire lane in front. Curly snatches the Five-Points rack of water for Mars. Benny opens the door and grabs his rack. Dooby jumps out, slamming his face into the icy ground from the unexpected drop and sprints to the door wagging his tail like a hummingbird. This lucky mongrel is the only happy thing at this ominous high school. Even our principal, Mr. Sweeney, has given up on us. All he does is run to his office to drink and read novels. He hasn't stepped foot in the Activities Hall in years. If we do see an adult, it's our Assistant Principal visiting our hot gym teacher. These guys don't have to worry about shit because there are no helicopter parents in this town. "Ash High, where dreams go to die."

Irish is a bull among calves upon his entrance into the Activities Hall. Two hooded freshmen open the school doors. Ash High is similar

8

to walking into the Roman Coliseum, except instead of gladiators and lions, it's boys and lionesses. Curly picks up Dooby. Shea walks in first. Benny and Curly follow, waiting for us to enter before heading to their respective Quarter benches. Irish drops a cig stick into an old army canteen, pulls out an unlit cig stick, and rests it in his left ear. He follows me in.

Lights flicker like flames. The Activities Hall echoes with cackles and chatter like that of hyenas surrounding a zebra. A curl of overdone cologne, perfume, and smoked weed permeates the air. My skin turns to goosebumps stepping into the Hall. Everyone covers their faces with hoods. It feels like walking into an evil monastery.

The ceiling reaches at least fifty feet high and brick walls spread a football field wide. The floors are the same color as the brick outside. Benches or "Quarters" are on the sides. Not a soul stands in the middle.

On the walls are enormous flat screens that mock us in repeated loops of past Powder Match highlights. It's an old, traditional competition with our rivals, the Cherries of Cherry Ridge. It's reached world-wide attention and the winner gets the money from pay-per-view listings. We need the money in order for Ashton to survive. The Powder Match includes: Academia, consisting of five events (Applied Mathematics, Music, Chemistry, Art and Literature); The Chute, a dramatic downhill snow competition; and a climactic Snow Brawl used to break any tie. We have to win this year. We win and we get enough money to support our town.

Over and over we're stuck watching re-runs of highlights from my dad winning the Academia trial. That's my event. Academia is the first event in the Powder Match. We'd have a shot, but Twitch and I have been our only representatives for the past three years. We lose Academia because our school still uses chalkboards, while the Cherries have the most modern of learning tools.

Vivian Steele has won the second event, the Chute, three years in a row.

We're surrounded by highlights of the original Irish, Jimmy Punch, and his Smoke Quartermate, Mickey Slay, Twitch and Irish's dad, taking down Cherries on the Snow Brawl pitch. We used to win all the time. Not anymore.

Irish couldn't fight last year in the final event, the Snow Brawl. He was hospitalized, after standing up to Mickey. Mickey doesn't touch Twitch, so his alcoholic beatings are double when he gets to Irish. Irish is locked down when it comes to that stuff, so I stopped asking him about it.

We've literally been getting our asses kicked for years in the Snow Brawl. This is it. Now it's our turn. It has to be.

Dooby growls at the screens and Curly pets him, lifting his ear to whisper, "Maybe one day, Dooby. One day." Curly puts Dooby on the floor to waddle to the Special Ed. area where he spends the day as a therapy dog.

Irish walks through the doors and our show begins. Chatter halts and eyes glue to his every step.

He stops at Mars's quarter.

Mars, thin, tall, and dark, wears his hood tight and sleek jeans that show lean muscle. The Five-Points Quarter is full of jocks and carries the most noise in the Hall. If there's any legit party, it's in Five-Points. With a slick shake of the hand (a Five-Points signature), Mars says, "There's my man. Yo, Irish, I gotta give you props for taking care of shit this weekend. I don't know what my moms would've done if she found out Berries came by our spot. We would have had trouble like that in a minute for sure. Anything you need… Points got yo back." He crunches his knuckles looking around the room, nervous. "You too, J. I ain't ever heard a boy stick it to a Berry like that. That's some smooth ass shit you were spitting to those Cops about warrants. Them bitches was out in five. Appreciate it, fam."

I say, "No worries, Mars, cops are always crooked in your neck. Your sister is coming in this year, right?"

He glances over our shoulders when the doors open. "Yeah, yeah… she'll be here in a bit, right quick. Been up since four this morning, ya know. I keep telling her shit'll be fine, but she can't get the first day of the Hall rumors out of her head, I guess."

"She'll be fine, M. No one's gonna say anything with her being *your* sister. It'll be a walk in the park."

"Word, word." He pats me on the back. "I'll catch you two at the Bridge later."

"If we make it back from Cherry Ridge," I say.

"Shit. It's that time of the month again. Damn."

"For sure. It's *that* time of year."

Curly's Quarter is a bunch of crunchy, hippie stoners talking about new strains of weed or their hallucinations from the past weekend's trip. I don't know what is stronger; the dank smell of weed, the stale smell of smoked weed, or the lack of soap and B. O. derant. Irish doesn't care, so he heads to Benny's Quarter.

Benny's Freshmore bench is so terrified and awestruck of just being on the bench that they act like it's the first day of kindergarten.

Irish moves to his Q1 recliner next to the top bench. It's really two benches in one.

One is the top boy, the other the top girl.

It's not just a bench, it's a birthright. Only the elite from every Quarter has a chance to sniff the aroma of the Q1's. In order to be a Q1, you're either a lucky kid to be allowed through close friendships (like me), have something unique to offer Ash as a school (like me), or you're a legacy (like me).

I need a drink.

When Ash first opened, the Q1's were jocks and cheerleaders. Now it's made up of the school's winners of all kinds. Well, mostly winners. The Nerds don't sniff the Hall.

Vivian, the top girl of the school, sits on her bench with her Chicklets. She'll do pretty much anything to keep it that way. Irish and I have tried to convince her to allow some Nerds in the Hall for Academia, but she prefers her own pawns for Academia and the Snow Brawl pitch. Since she's our representative in this year's Chute, a single person competition, she has the most power in the election process. Doesn't help that Vivian is forced on Irish because she's Bart Steele's daughter. I hate that we need her.

Her voice snakes through the air as we approach. "Hey, Ish! You're lookin' fine today."

Every time she screeches it makes my skin crawl. It's like hearing teeth grind against concrete. I don't know if it's her painted-on pants or low-cut tank top accenting her tanned boob job, or maybe it's even the way she sits with her legs crossed, like she's too good for the rest of us, but it's almost impossible *not* to be pissed off by her presence.

I try to focus on her overdone face paint to clear my mind. She probably would have beautiful eyes if they weren't caked with the entire make-up aisle. There's always something about that fake tan line surrounding the brim of her chin that draws attention to hidden blemishes of acne on her cheeks.

"Hey, Vivian," I say.

She looks at her newly done nails.

"Jester."

I look to her top Chicklet and say, "Hey, Chirp."

"Hey! J.!"

Vivian shoots a sharp look to her right. "Bitch! I say you could talk?"

Poor Chirp has always been Vivian's side-chick. She'd probably be a top girl at any other school. She's just as pretty as the other girls. Just because she's from Five-Points and in honors classes doesn't mean she should be treated like that. I don't know why she takes it. Ashton can do this to you.

Irish sits down on the leather recliner. I stand next to him.

"Irish? You're gonna talk to me this year? I'm your Queen," Vivian says.

He sniffs at her.

Vivian flips her hair and turns to Chirp. "Go get me my latte from the cafe!"

Chirp looks down and under her breath says, "Yes, Vivian. Sorry, Vivian."

The other girls on the bench look like they're from Vivian's favorite magazine, *Laramie*. They don't say shit unless they're allowed to. They're probably more talented and beautiful than Vivian, but because her sister was a past Winter Olympics snowboard star, she's pretty much been in line for Queen for years.

The morning bell rings.

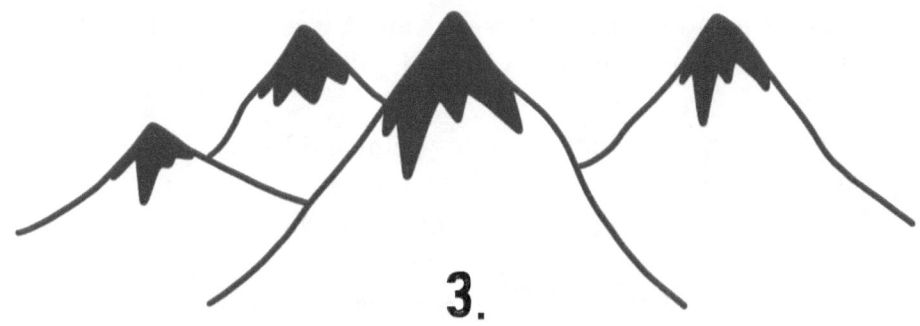

3.

THE GAUNTLET

CONVERSATIONS OF SUMMER parties and exploits come to a halt, and the minions of the Quarters pull out their phones.

The first door opens. I hate this part.

A petite freshman girl walks through; can't be more than five feet tall. Her backpack wraps around her like she's about to climb Snowdrop Peak. It's Harp Skye, a Nerd with the voice of an angel. Her jeans have rips scattered around her thighs. She's cute, with long brown hair to her waist, noticeable in the chest and trying to show it off with a low-cut blouse. Her fear is expressed in every step as she creeps down the Hall trying to disguise the clopping of her heels.

Eyes stick to her every move like prey being eyed by creatures in a forest. When she passes, each bench blasts their phones, giving her a score.

This sucks.

Interrupting the silence, a Fresh-ass from Benny's Quarter screams out, "Damn! Look at them titties!" Benny jacks him in the jaw. Benny doesn't carry much power amongst the Brigade. He's younger, smaller, and his hoodie is big on him. It looks like he is swimming in it. But in the Hall, things are different.

The little girl can only trudge past each bench staring at the floor knowing she's cheap steak at the meat market.

She finishes and stands before Irish and Vivian. Each Q1 is reading their texts from the Quarters and sending their responses for the final evaluation.

The group message vibrates in my palm and I show it to Irish.

He gives a nod.

The screens in the hall switch to black. A white 6 flashes, followed by downward thumbs.

The little girl looks at Irish. She tilts her head in respect with tears in her eyes. We just look at her in silence. Like wussies. She turns left down the Academic Hall. My phone vibrates with texts from Benny, Curly, and Mars showing an 8.

Shea texts me: **Damn bro... Vivian gave her a six? She was a solid 7... especially for a Nerd. She's better than that, right?!**

I can't really do much but shrug my shoulders. I thought she was a solid 9. Vivian's cold-hearted, though. I text him back: **I got 8's from the Q's. Screw Vivian. 30 more minutes of this shit.**

One after another, Vivian selects pawns for the Snow Brawl pitch and hands a bottle of water to each Quarter, or they're sent down the Academic Hall. I just sit, watch, and speak for Irish. After so many "declinations for the hall," I put my head in my hands and get ready for the next bit of hell.

Air sucks out of the Hall.

Shea texts: **Guess who Mars found...?**

He points to two towering kids. One's a six-foot wrecking ball, the other a seven-foot tree.

I text: **Who are they?**

Shea texts: **Just moved in to Five Points. Cousins.**

They walk together with confidence. The Hall stands as they pass. Irish stands as they approach.

"What are your names?" I ask.

They say nothing, put their heads down, and walk towards the Five-Points Quarter. Mars's right hand, a kid named Leon, jumps up in a dramatic fashion, brushing manicured hair from his eyes and says, "Whoa, Whoa, Whoa!" He push-turns the Cousins across the Hall towards us and speaks, scared.

Leon says, "Sorry, Irish, they're new and don't really understand. Butter and Scotch Riley are their names. They can offer assistance in the Snow Brawl."

Irish sits down next to a case of water.

Holding in my excitement because maybe I won't die this year, I say, "So they're going to fight for us?"

"With you. Jester, sir," Scotch says.

"Okay. We got it," I say.

I hand them two red Five-Point hoodies. They walk down the hall and numbers from 8 through 10 flash across the screens for them. They sit on the Five-Points bench.

The door opens with about five minutes left before class. Just a few more sentencings.

Neveah enters. Her body curves like it's sculpted from marble. She's wearing a tight-fitted Kelly green Ash shirt that highlights the insane color of her eyes. Two big magnificent emeralds. The Hall silences. I don't know if it's because of her beauty, or just the fact that she's Mars's sister. It doesn't matter, because 10's show on the screen before she reaches us.

She steps before Irish. He places two fingers on his right temple and waves in the direction of Mars's quarter. As she begins to take a few steps to his bench, Vivian raises her hand.

"Excuse me! Don't I get a say in this?"

Mars's bench grumbles, most of which consists of, "Screw that trick, bitch." Mars stands up to shut them up. They shut up.

Vivian sends a text to Chirp's phone, locking eyes at Mars with a conniving smirk. Chirp walks towards me and presents her phone. I show Irish the phone.

He looks at the ground for a few seconds, coughs twice, and rolls the unlit cig stick between his fingers. To the Hall, the seconds feel like watching an hourglass. He pats me on the back. I stand up.

I announce: "The women of Q1 are offering an invitation for Neveah Beamo—"

Before I can finish the sentence, a roar punches the walls in protest and fury. I can't recognize what they're saying.

Mars sits like stone and lets them rage. After about a minute of deafening noise, he slides his hood off. Without bothering to look to his messenger, he speaks. "We'll accept the offer on one condition. We get Christmas Daye."

In a snap, the Hall turns to murmurs saying, "Christmas Daye? For real?"

Christmas, or Christi as I like to call her, is also a senior. She's one of the first girls ever to be a first-year Q1 without being a legacy. She's a top snowboarder, captain cheerleader, academic scholar, and top-shot for next year's Winter Olympics Team. She's different from all the other girls. It helps that she's pretty, but she's so much more than that. She's strong. I'm terrified of her. I've had her in a few classes and she's just perfect. It doesn't hurt that her dad played for the Denver Broncos.

Still, I don't know if Vivian's going to give up Christi for a freshman from Five-Points. Before she can speak, Irish eliminates any chance of contention. He accepts her with two fingers to the temple.

When Neveah finally reaches Vivian, the only thing she receives is a cold-ass dismissive handshake. The two girls' eyes slightly meet, but dart straight to the floor.

Shea shoots me a quick text. **Well... things just stepped up a notch.**

I text: **Vivian is jealous as shit dude. It's just cause she wants all the attention in the match.**

When Christi gets off the bench, she spends minutes getting hugs and kisses from the girls, like she's being drafted to war. Five-Points may be poor as hell and have some sketchy neighborhoods, but it's not that bad if you're in Mars's Quarter. She still gets to go to the Bridge. That's good. I'm going to miss her though. Damn.

Christi's flip-flops are inches high and click after each step. Not a person in the Hall could have conceived a trade like this happening, let alone knowing how to react when witnessing it. She approaches the Five-Points Quarter terrified, but still raises her head to meet them. Most of the bench eyes her up and down, some looking the other way, acting as if they ignore her very existence.

Leon says, "Shit, girl, we just be playin' wit ya. You don't wanna be wit those tricks anyways. We take care of our people over here in the Points. Girls, move aside and make a place for Miss Christmas right here."

One girl abstains and says, "I ain't movin.'"

Leon snaps his fingers at her. "Girl, I wasn't asking."

The girl gives a wisp of disgust and moves over. When Christi sits down, Leon examines every part of her in an instant.

"Girl, you gorgeous. Now I got competition for being the most beautiful in school." Christmas gives a giggle. "See girl, that's that smile we all been watching."

He brushes strands of hair from her face.

"Shiite. Wit my help. You gonna be the prettiest girl in the Olympics."

A light comes to Christi's face as she looks to Leon and asks, "You know about the Olympics?"

"Hell, yeah girl! You kidding me? I've seen some of those videos online. You're crazy."

"Ha… yeah I guess, but I dunno, I'm kind of a long shot right now."

"Hell, no you ain't! You've come home to the Points now. We ain't like those Q1 bitches. We got yo back, girl."

Silence again takes over the Hall.

Shea: **Well who's next? The President's daughter? Ha.**

Me: **Shit… hope not… Vivian would start a Civil War… ha-ha.**

The five-minute bell rings. Last one.

A taller girl, older than a freshman for sure, enters with a delicate closing of the door. She recognizes the silence and attempts to close the door without a sound. When she turns around, the look on her face is that of an actress who forgot her lines on Opening Night. She turns left, but is stopped by a massive wall. She turns right and is halted by the lock of the cafeteria doors. Her only option is forward, through the Gauntlet.

I don't notice at first, but as she passes Mars's and Curly's bench it's obvious. It's *her*. My neighbor's daughter.

She walks straight and in a proper manner, grasping six books to her chest like a kinder-grader. Her hair is shiny black, pulled up into a ponytail. She's hidden behind academic glasses wearing a sky-colored V-neck sweater with a white collared undershirt, which blows up her highlight-blue eyes. Her jeans have an unbuttoned top button showing a brief view of her panty line. Every eye sticks to her like a tongue frozen to a pole.

I elbow Irish, but he's already staring in a trance. I've never seen this look on him. It's like he's staring at a ghost. Or a celebrity. Maybe a celebrity ghost. Their eyes meet.

I don't know what causes it, a shoelace, or seeing Irish for the first time, but she trips and falls to the ground. Along with her books and journals sprawling across the floor, the stomachs and hearts of the Hall fall with her.

She picks up the books in desperation, bending every which way, trying to hold her tears. No one moves. She bends over towards the Q1 bench. A hint of her panty-line creases under her jeans. Vivian sneers with a vicious screech, "Nice Granny panties!"

At first, the giggles feel forced from the Q1 Chicklets, but while the girl continues to pick up papers and journals, the entire Hall echoes with waves of laughter.

She reaches for the final book, Fitzgerald's *The Great Gatsby*. Just as she's about to grasp the cover, a large hand clasps the book.

The laughter stops as Irish helps her up and hands her the book.

Their eyes come together, his showing embrace, hers defense.

Speechless, he stares at her as she escapes.

He wrenches me off the bench after her. I throw the phone at Shea as I'm dragged like a doll through the East Hall. My last glimpse is of Shea, looking at his phone, wide-eyed, and the screen above him showing… 10.

Irish's hand wraps my forearm like a bear trap and sends a searing pain into my shoulder with each step.

Jesus man. It's just another girl.

I try to apologize to passing students, but the speed and pain are jarring. The crowd finally dissipates like Spaniards in The Running of the Bulls. We pass full classrooms without teachers. From substitute no-shows to teachers that just don't show, monkeys hang from rafters in this zoo.

We begin to approach the Academic Hall and she appears walking alone with her head down.

Like a train about to stop, Irish halts his pace, and my entire body is thrown forward. The steel trap tightens. He catches me mid-air, almost tearing my arm from its shoulder socket.

"What's your name?" he asks her.

She stops, but doesn't turn to respond.

"Jester, what's her name?" he asks.

"I don't know, Irish. She's new. A couple of days maybe."

The Academic Hall stalls from held breath. It's rare to see anyone from the Activities Hall in this part of school, let alone Irish. The tension is an amalgamation of anxiety, fear, and intrigue. His nails dig into the flesh of my forearm. The pain subsides by my own curiosity. She stands frozen, staring at her feet, again grasping her books to her chest.

His fingers slowly release one by one, leaving indents in my skin. His hand trembles as he reaches to her shoulder.

The bell for first period rings.

Students rush in a frenzy desperately fighting to get to class on time. Irish doesn't move.

Scattered with stray pens and pencils, a few sticky notes roll across the floor. The tardy bell rings. I tap him on the shoulder.

"Hey man… I gotta get to… I mean… I should get to class. You gonna be all right?"

He doesn't say a word.

"Irish? You gonna be all right?"

Nothing.

I've known him my whole life and have never seen him like this. I strike him and holler, "Reginald!"

He throws me against a locker, and raises my body off the ground to meet his eyes.

My legs squirm. It's futile.

A tear drops from the corner of my left eye. He follows it down the side of my cheek. As it falls off my chin towards the floor, he releases his grip and drops me. My throat is scalding. Fighting through the burn, I burst, "What the shit, dude?!"

He slams his fist into the locker next to my face. Shock takes over. My mind turns blank.

I wake to Irish screaming, "J.?!… J.?!… Jester!… C'mon!? Wake up, man!"

I try to push myself up, but my arm gives out. He stands me up. His eyes moisten. He scans the hall to see if anyone is around and whispers, "Hey man… are you okay? I don't know what happened. Did I do this?"

Well, I didn't do it.

I want to kill him. But the fury settles as I see our roles reversed. His body trembles and tears stream from both eyes. I don't know what to say. I let it pass.

"It's okay, man," I say.

He takes my hand, lifts me up, and says, "Never again, man, I promise. Next round at the Bridge is on me."

I massage my throat.

"Don't worry about it. I think it's best I just get to class."

"Word… take this." He hands me a stolen tardy pass. "I'll see ya at the Bridge then?"

"For sure."

Before we separate, he makes sure to give me an of bottle of water he's been hiding in his hoodie pouch for Twitch and says, "Make sure, Twitch gets this."

Twitch is a brilliant artist. He *used* to be our Smoke Quartermate. Curly was forced to replace him after last year's Powder Match. While Irish was in the hospital, Twitch had to be his replacement in the Snow Brawl. He can't fight. The Cherry King, Sonny Gatson, made sure he never touched the Powder Match again by beating him to a pulp. Those shit-holes will do anything to win.

Irish and I head in opposite directions.

I go to the bathroom to clean myself up.

I empty the container of soap to scrub away the smell of cig sticks, put in eye drops, and then chug some Listerine. I peel off some skin where Irish's nails dug into me. A good thing because it takes that much time for my eye drops to hide my liquor-eyes. Can't be anything worse than showing up to class fifteen minutes late on the first day of school looking wasted.

There's actually a difference between being tardy and being late to class. Every kid runs in a couple minutes tardy now and then, but I'm going on fifteen minutes at least. Before I open the door, I take a deep breath, turn the knob, and receive countless interrupted eyes. I'll never get over how awkward it is to walk into an IB classroom late. It's like I'm walking into *their* temple.

IB stands for International Baccalaureate, a balanced program of advanced college courses, one of which is Art History.

I find the room: IB-505.

Perfect. The class is still working on a lame "get-to-know-you" exercise. I can't see the teacher, but I find Twitch. He's sitting alone, rolling a strand of rope between his fingers. I give him his bottle.

"Twitch, you wouldn't be able to point out Ms. Madonna? Would you?" I ask.

He points to the back corner of the room with his chin glued to his chest.

I follow his finger expecting to see a typical IB teacher: grey, married, with kids, drives a Buick. She's covering a class syllabus, which includes studying Michelangelo, Matisse, and Degas. But the sight of her will be etched in my memory forever. It's the woman from the walk of shame this morning. The class is pointless. The only things I study are the curves under her dress.

I usually head to the Bridge for a beer at lunch, but the rollercoaster of emotions from the morning events have drained me. I take the afternoon off.

4.

THE CHERRIES

POWDER MATCH: 56 DAYS

I'T'S FRIDAY.
After dinner, I jump down the stairs, put on some slippers, and bolt to the door. Mom has poured herself a full glass of wine and has already gone through a bottle as she works on a 1,000-piece puzzle. She's been working on it for months now. Solving puzzles helps prevent her PTSD episodes. I wish I could just walk out the door, but Doobs catches me. I pat her on the head. Irish will freak out if I keep him waiting, so I act as casual as possible.

"Hey Mom. I'm headed out for bit," I say.

C'mon Mom. Tell me not to go.

"Okay. Have a good ti—wait, it's 9:00! Where the hell are you going so late?" she says.

"Just to the Hill for a bit with Irish and the fellas. Shouldn't be too late."

"Dammit! I can't figure out this smoke coming from the factory," she says, studying the puzzle.

This is a time I wish I *had* a mom.

"Yeah, Mom. Thanks. Love ya."

"Damn, smoke," she says.

"You're almost there Mom."

As I enter the limo, cig stick-soaked air pours down my throat, and I can't help hacking. Shea sits up front with Benny, and Irish is alone in back.

After my throat clears, I ask Irish, "What's up, man?"

He doesn't say a word. There's no music. He rolls up the window. The engine growls and away we roll. It's the only sound for the next ten minutes.

What's going on? Why is it so quiet?

We approach the last red light before the turn towards the Dam. The Dam, a couple hundred feet high, towers through the valley, separating two massive lakes. It stretches to Cherry Ridge and Snowdrop Resort, eventually reaching to the outside world through a tunnel on the southeastern side. Cherry Ridge controls the Dam; the Ashton side is nearly dry.

Irish lights up a cig stick as I grab a beer. The smoke swirls passing streetlights as he looks down. He blows the last remains of his cig stick out the left side of his mouth and says, "You weren't at the Bridge."

I knew it was coming. I flick the tab of the can and take a sip.

"Oh… yeah… I wasn't feeling too well. My—"

With a slight scoff and light slap to my face, he barrels a laugh and holds the back of my head, pulling our foreheads together. Irish says, "Ha… Connelly. You're the best Jester an Irish could ask for."

As we creep to the top of the Dam, we pass the bullet-riddled, rusted Tincup sign, a ghost town a hundred miles to the west. We finally reach the Dam's peak. There's not a drug in the world that can match the feeling of being on the Dam.

The night swallows us and the milky moonlight moves with wind-blown clouds. Stars glitter against the velvet sky.

The limo turns the final corner to the Dam and slows to a halt at the gate. Beams of white light engulf the car. Benny rolls the window down and asks Irish, "Sir?"

Lights still flashing, there's a gentle knock on my window. I roll the window down a few inches so only I meet the eyes outside. As expected, it's Clove, the gate guard. The only acceptable Cherry. Fit and

23

big, Clove's skin is olive and natural, as opposed to other Cherries who spend their lives under a scalpel.

Hesitant, he asks, "What's up, J.?"

"Not much, Clove, how you been, man?"

With a heavy, sarcastic breath, he responds, "Just living the dream."

"Your Rents?"

"Fake Dad's a piece of shit, as you know, never around, cheating on Mom when he found out she was sick. Any sign of Jimmy? Mom always asks about him and my sister."

"Sorry, Clove. He's bailed. We still don't know what happened."

Well, we know what happened. Jimmy burnt his own house down and bailed on Ashton.

I reach a few fingers through the gap, give him a shake, and say, "Sorry to hear that, man."

Irish hands me a 100-bag of Sweets. I say, "These are a special batch specifically for your mom from the factory. No addiction. No cure. No pain."

"Appreciate it, J., but the cops will kill me if they find out I helped you guys."

"Look, Clove, these Sweets are yours either way, but we're getting through that gate. It's up to you how."

He draws a few anxious breaths, and using a remote, opens the gate. He reaches his hand in the window, we exchange the bag, and before I let go, I say, "Sucks you're a Cherry, Clove. Always liked ya."

We enter Cherry Ridge, and even for me, it's hard not to be shocked at the site of the Garden and the Cherries' bubble gum mansions. Lit in magnificent colors mimicking the most beautiful flowers in the world, each compound constructed in quartz, diamond, glass, or emerald is designed to display each family's wealth. Clove's clover-shaped house is closest to the Dam.

Each house ignites when we pass. The neighborhood escalates in gaudiness as we reach the Elites.

Once we reach them, we park down in the woods next to Powder Lake and the Lillys' massive 200 ft. yacht connected to a long cement pier. We leave Benny in the car. Shea, Irish, and I exit the limo. After a few hundred yards, we approach the house. I hate to admit it, but I have always liked the Lillys' mansion. Entwined in translucent tubes stocked with exotic fish, the mansion looks like a giant, liquid funnel cake. I have always given them a pass considering they've been gone for years trying to fix the drought in the southwest. We have to pass their place to get to Sonny.

The Lillys' house is majestic and it's the most dangerous to intruders. The back lawn is mowed close like a golf green. A stray shoelace falls from the tip of my shoe across the edge of their lawn. Shea pulls me back.

Hundreds of pipes shoot like arrows out of the ground. Six-foot-tall hydrants spew boiling water. We only get few minutes of warm water for a shower in Ashton, so the heat stings. Water vapor and steam cloud the lawn. I don't know how we're going to get through without our skin blistering.

Sketch.

"Zip up your hoods," Irish commands.

Shea says, "Shit, thank god our hoods are impermeable."

"Geez, Shea," Irish says, "You deal with this all the time? Buzz kill."

Shea finds the path to Cherry Ridge without being noticed. He spits his toothpick to the ground and sprints, slaloming like a skier through the mazes of water. We copy his every move.

Irish is hit in the face. He doesn't react.

Drops hit my face and sting like a swarm of bees.

We approach the side of the mansion, scale the steel fence, and escape the blasts of scalding water.

The sidewalk is lined with barren trees that make a cocoon of spikes and a death tube to encase trespassers. The trees fold around Irish, trapping him.

We hear branches break every step of the way. Irish blasts through bloody and torn. He remains focused and ignores the shock on our faces.

Sonny's mansion looks like a glamorous "White House" made of white gold. Sonny is the King of the Cherries.

Irish commands, "No matter what you see, hear, or feel, don't remove your hood, or say a word. Sonny already knows we're here. He's going to look for any weakness.

5.

SONNY

THE AIR IS SO CRISP, cold, and clean that we share a cough together. Irish hands Shea and I cig sticks to recover and jokes, "Jesus, how do they breathe up here?"

After a slight chuckle, Irish leads, and we follow into the Snowdrop Village.

Not nearly as overdone as the Garden, the Village looks like a nostalgic mountain-time from the early millennium. Storefronts are fashioned from old oak, pine, aspen, and blends of beetle kill.

Lights off so we can't see, but I know when open, these shops are carcass sellers. Not only leather, they'll pay for any animal they can find, endangered or not, including illegal laboratory hybrids they've made on their own.

Ice flakes fall serene and melt on the heated brick from Cherry snow blowers as we head to the base of Snowdrop Resort. Meeting the cross point in the village, we turn left, and cackles of sloppy laughter and loud music reverberate through the buildings. Irish stops Shea from taking another step forward. He and I lead, Shea follows.

We approach the base and it's exactly as expected. We see teenagers gulping liquor shooters from ice chutes and sculptures. Chasing each other with inflated balloons, fighting and laughing, they puke in barrels like the privileged drug-crazed children they are. It's like witnessing a toddler's birthday party with the guests tripping on hallucinogens.

My mom is a saint compared to the Cherry parents. Cherries are so busy counting their money, they let their kids do anything.

Sonny's minions don't notice us until the music turns off.

They turn on us forming a disorganized barricade in front of Sonny's slope-side cabin that's bigger than my house. A gondola exits the backside of his cabin and carries empty chairs into the blackness of Snowdrop Peak.

Sonny stands wearing a bright pink snow suit. His face has been through enough surgeries that it's as smooth as a plastic doll's. His chiseled features flow into a chin with a dimple so pronounced that the front of his jaw looks like a butt. It's been months since we've last seen each other; he looks stronger than I could have imagined. More massive than Irish, his frame fills the Cherry throne resting on the front balcony. Steam wafts from the basin of hot water his feet rest in.

As he leans with his head held back, a few Cherry snow maidens help to reveal his locks of gold. He checks his manicured nails, waits for Daisy, the Cherry Queen, to season and cut his steak before she feeds it to him.

Daisy's suit mimics Sonny's, except hers is white with a pink trim that is skin tight on her voluptuous curves. I can't imagine it's easy for her to buy clothes with curves like that.

I'm not going to lie. Daisy is pretty hot. She is what Vivian tries to be. A Barbie doll.

After a swallow, he lifts his feet from the basin and doesn't look at us when he speaks.

"Well, look who it is. Why do I have the pleasure of meeting the infamous Irish and his ever so clever Jester?"

"Sonny. You know why we're here," I say.

Sonny wants our Sweets. Our Sweets are unique to the market. They're non-addictive painkillers. Our Sweets can be used as steroids, and in some cases can even cure dementia or Alzeheimer's. Mixy Combow, a Nerd, and her parents come up with the concoctions. We have been forced to sell a special batch to Sonny for the Powder Match.

He waves Daisy off and looks at us with mocking inquisition. "Why, whatever do you mean?"

Irish jumps forward, but Sonny pushes his palm to the air and stops him. "Nope, this is my side of the valley. Know your place, brute."

He leans back in his chair and flicks his wrist at his snow maidens. They present a large glass bowl full of Sweets from the factory. Stroking his dimpled chin, he asks himself, "Now, now, what kind of Ash should I be tonight?" He pulls out a brown chocolate ball and says, "Maybe I'll be a Five-Point," and tosses it in his mouth, chewing it ever so softly before swallowing.

"You know, Irish" he says, "historians may be right about Mars's ancestors being bred to be nothing more than machines and servants."

Racist ass.

Sonny reaches in the bowl again and says, "Nah, that's boring. Maybe I'll throw a little euphoria in the mix and go wild like the Vikings. What do you think Curly would say about that?"

With a demonic giggle, Sonny reaches deep into the bowl for a black, hard candy. "Maybe tonight I'll just be an Irish and beat the hell out of everyone."

Daisy pours a glass of wine for him to finish the candy off, but before he can, I say, "You mean suck *off* the Irish?"

Sonny chokes.

I say, "Sorry, Sonny… everyone knows the Irish candy is the hardest. I didn't know you enjoyed sucking off a hard Irish."

Sonny's cheeks flare with rage. He jumps off the ledge of his balcony to land right in front of me where we glare face to face. Irish grabs his throat and throws him to the ground, forcing him to spit the candy from his mouth, and says, "What? Speechless, Sonny?"

His minions charge towards us, but Sonny raises his hand to stop them.

"That's enough, Irish," I say. He lets Sonny up.

Massaging his throat, Sonny says, "You got our Sweets, Jester?"

"You got the money, Sonny?"

He tosses a briefcase of cash. We open it and look inside. There's enough cash to feed our town. Almost.

Irish, Shea, and I walk back through the village. Before we turn the corner, Sonny shouts, "Oh, Irish, how is Twitch, by the way?"

Shit, Irish. Don't do it. Twitch can't be fixed. We need you healthy for the Powder Match.

Irish turns and runs towards Sonny. Sonny speeds towards Irish. Before they collide, Irish moves to his left, straightens his right arm, and collars Sonny. Sonny flips backwards and lands on the ground losing his breath. Irish pummels his face and chest with his elbows. Sonny's minions run to take Irish off him. Shea and I do the same. As we pull him away, he finishes by kicking Sonny in the balls.

Sonny rolls around in agony, trying to catch his breath. His minions pick him up and carry him up the stairs. They sit him on his throne.

Daisy screams, "Get out Ash Trays!"

A siren sounds.

I pull my hood over my head and we bolt down the street. I wonder how we're going to make our way through the water-maze and back to the limo.

Before exiting the village, Shea stops us and we huddle up. He presents me a piece of paper.

"What's this?" I ask.

Shea says, "It's an exit map my dad gave me, so we don't have to go through the neighborhoods."

"Give it here," I say.

I read the map. We have to go through Cherry Ridge High School.

Cherry Ridge High School is a complex of three buildings, each the size of Ash High. The campus is surrounded by a massive ropes course. Each Cherry gets a collection of teachers and classrooms at their disposal. The ropes course is used for training for the Powder Match, particularly the Snow Brawl.

I regard the intimidating tangle of ropes, towers, and platforms. "*This* is supposed to be easier?" I ask.

"Safer," Irish says.

"Okay. It is closer. And we can jet across to get to the Dam."

We run to the school. The campus is massive. Ashton High has maybe 2,000 kids; this place can school at least 4,000. It's swallowed in rope like a spider waiting in its web and about to pounce.

Shea points to a specific strand of rope near the base of the fence and hands Irish a blade. Irish cuts the strand and ropes collapse to the ground.

I say, "I think we're supposed to use the rope. I mean… it covers the whole courtyard."

Irish slaps my arm with a smirk of approval. My palms sweat for the next drink. And I salivate for what waits for me in the limo.

We walk on the icy rope and reach the base of the lake where we scramble into the limo. It's still filled with stale cig stick smoke. Irish hits the window, the engine rumbles, and we exit to the Dam entrance. Reaching the Dam barricade, I give Clove another 100-bag.

I shake his hand and say, "We won't forget tonight."

The limo window closes. Irish and I sit in silence. I fix me a drink and come back to normal. We reach the end of the Dam and head down into the darkness of Ashton.

We head up to the Hill, a meet up for the Irish Brigade. We cross through Five-Points and up the side of the mountain near Irish's house.

The Hill is scarred with new streets and half-completed million dollar houses. The Cherries have been fighting for this land for years. Gentrification is inevitable without money. Just another reason we have to win the Powder Match this year. Money to remake the town like we want.

"Give us some time," Irish commands Shea. Shea leaves the limo for a smoke.

I pour myself another drink.

He starts. "Another one?"

I say, "It's not like everybody is a saint in this valley. Cherries take whippets every day. So I have a drink every once in a while. Get off my back."

"J., it's turning into more than 'every once in a while.'"

"Screw off, Irish. Look at the shit life we live."

He pounds me in the shoulder.

"J., we need to start thinking about after high school. How am I going to provide for my people without the throne of Ash High? We can't just get by cutting wood and sketch dealings at the factory. We *need* the money from the Powder Match."

I scoff and point to my face saying, "You mean the games that gave me this scar."

It wasn't his fault. He wasn't there. Dammit, J.

"Sorry… Mickey really took the pressure out on me," Irish says.

"I know, Irish. My bad. Some days are just tougher than others in Ashton, you know."

"Yeah, I know. That's why we have the Hill."

Irish pulls an old military flashlight from the glove box. I look at him and he's already looking at me with a cheeky grin.

"Let's screw wit em'…" I say.

The horizon illuminates in white after Benny hits the high-beams like it's a drug raid. We exit the limo and see Mars and Curly ruffling around. It's hysterical, but the sketchy murmurs of, "What the hell, Dude?" and, "What do we do, man?" are even better.

I hold a flashlight as straight as possible. We exit the car resembling Berries. Cops. We slam the doors screaming, "Put your hands up!!"

A group of hands shoot up. Squinting at the light, the fellas are unable to see.

They scream and start pleading apologies, thinking it was the clicking of a gun, but it's Irish opening a can of sparkling water. He can't even take a full sip without spewing in laughter.

Wiping a tear from his eye, in mock, he yells, "Oh, c'mon, ya fairies… get the hell up! We aint gonna bite ya."

He grabs beers from a case inside the limo and waits for them to creep up. He tosses a beer to both Curly and Mars. Still blinded, they juggle and drop each can. Benny turns the lights off.

Two cans snap and Mars says, "Screw that sketchy shit, Irish. I be having to deal with them racist Berry and Cherry assholes every day."

Curly follows suit, wiping grass off his sweatshirt. "Ya, bruh… I'm on my second strike already with Cops. That's why Jimmy left."

Jimmy Punch is a former Irish Powder Match champion. My dad was his Jester. Jimmy took care of this town for years before his house caught fire. I think he was trying to bridge the gap between Ashes and Cherries by marrying a Cherry and having twins, but it made things worse. He disappeared with his daughter years ago after burning his house down. When Jimmy left, Clove and his mom, Jameson, were left to fend for themselves in Cherry Ridge. There is no in between. It's the haves and have nots.

I say, "My bad for getting your knickers all up in a bunch. You should have seen your faces, though. Priceless."

They chug their cans, settle, and we lie down facing the sky.

The next minutes of silence are the most relaxing I've had all day, until it's broken by Irish still puzzled from our earlier conversation.

He says, "So, what was so bad that you couldn't get a beer at the Bridge for lunch all week? Seeing as you never turn down a drink."

Shea follows with the same question. "Yeah, man, you never miss a Bridge lunch. What's up?

Curly is already rolling the tip of a blunt with his lighter and takes a hit. Then takes a couple more, he hands it to me. I take a puff and my head clears. After another sip of beer, I start, "Well, you guys remember my new neighbor?"

Mars says, "Yeah, Shea texted me about that. Didn't you get caught creepin'?"

"Well, yeah, I guess. That was just the first part. First of all, I'm not creeping on *him*. He's only been there a few days and he's got a beautiful woman over every night. Plus, the one Monday morning was a solid 10 for sure. Body was out of control."

Irish comes in, "So what's the fuss about then?"

Curly coughs. "Bruh… doesn't he have a daughter? Maybe he saw her naked."

"What? Shut up… no… just let me talk," I say. "So I'm already 15 minutes late to class, right?"

Mars jumps in. "Why was you late?"

Telling a story to stoners is like reading to a class of kindergarteners.

"Dammit… does it matter? Anyways, so I'm already entering the class late, and they're doing some sort of first-day garbage, but there isn't a teacher in the room. Until I turn around and there she is…"

Irish says, "Who?"

Curly says, "The daughter?"

"Dammit, Curly! Will you get off the daughter!"

"I wish… ha… just kidding… my bad, bruh. Then who was it?"

"The woman I caught sneaking out of my neighbor's backyard that morning."

A breeze ruffles the nearby leaves.

"You know… the fine chick I saw in the buck."

It hits Irish. "Wait. The naked chick? Oh, that's dope."

The group rolls in laughter.

Mars catches his breath and says, "So let me get this straight. You got this fine-ass teacher that be gettin' loose the night before school… ha-ha… that shit could only happen to you, J…. for sure."

"You're telling me, man. The worst part was trying not to think of her naked and keepin' it down for the whole week. It was brutal."

Irish chimes in, "So that's why you didn't show? Because your teacher's hot?"

"No! I just needed some time on my own. Deal with stuff at home. Why is it so important anyways? It's not like anything changes at the Bridge. Let me guess… the Quarters had a few drinks and drove back to school."

Irish cracks each knuckle one by one.

"Or *did* something happen?" I ask the group.

Mars starts, "Man… shit was just awkward. Christmas sipped a water while everyone else looked at her in disgust while drinking malt liquor. No matter, man… she'll get warm… I got Leon handling them jealous bitches. Just first day shit, ya know. It's been awhile since Five-Points got a girl like her. She lightens shit up, if ya know what I'm saying. Vivian's still buggin' from earlier this week. Just sending nasty ass stares at Irish for that nerdy chick thing. She even came over and threw an entire glass of wine in his face. She's straight up two-bits psycho."

I nudge Irish with my elbow.

"Damn. For real? What the hell did you do?"

He stands up, rips out a bottle of water from his back pocket, and throws it unopened into the night.

Mars speaks for him. "Nothing… stood up and walked out. Every-one just sat around their booths drinking in silent whispers."

"That's sketch. Where were you during this, Curly?" I ask.

He doesn't say anything.

"Curly… Curly!"

"Huh… sorry bruh… I was just staring at the stars. It's crazy how they're so far away, ya know. What'd you say again?"

"Where was your Quarter during all this?"

"Ahhh… I didn't see anything. We just finished a bake in the parking lot, and we were walking in when Irish busted out the door and went straight to his limo. I dunno if it was because I was blitzed from the session, but it was mad sketch in there. We sat down for maybe a few minutes and I couldn't take it, so we bounced out."

Twisted from weed and beer, I blurt out, "Damn, Irish, and you didn't say anything to Vivian?"

Irish's eyes are black when he jolts to me. As I'm about to apologize, Mars saves me by asking Irish, "Speaking of that shit, what the hell happened with that nerdy chick? I mean she was cute and all, but damn, I ain't ever seen Vivian that pissed."

Irish remains still.

"She's my neighbor's daughter," I say.

Mars chokes in mid chug of his beer, spits it out, and asks, "Wait, so after all that other shit, the nerdy girl is your neighbor's daughter? No wonder you were screwed up this week. Still though, Irish, what was all that about?"

He speaks. "You heard what Jester said about her father. That house is messed up. She didn't deserve to be laughed at like that. I didn't even know she got a 10 until you told me during third period."

"Oh! That's right! I forgot about that," Mars says. "That was some crazy shit. She was cute… but a 10? That was a surprise for sure. She better not mess shit up."

Irish rips up dirt and releases it to the wind.

He says, "Yeah… I dunno… prolly just the fact that I helped her pick up her shit or something. She's from the Academic Hall anyways. It'll blow over. I don't really care to talk about it. Screw Vivian. Can we talk about something else?"

How about you almost killing me?

Curly, out of his drug coma, chimes in, "Yeah! I want to hear a Jester tale!"

Mars follows, "Yeah, for sure, man! And not one of the same old ones we've heard a million times. Something fresh."

34

Together, the Irish Brigade chants, "To him who speaks and protects the weak. To him who saves and carries our graves. Our Jester he be. We are blessed for thee."

I pull out a pint of Jameson that I'd pocketed while in the limo.

"Yeah... J. ... make us laugh," Irish says.

When I stand up, I get light-headed and every substance volleys through my brain. I'm loose. A little wobbly, I slur an old tale.

"All right... all right... I got one for ya."

I start. "First of all, you better not interrupt this time like a bunch of baby schoolers."

"Cool."

"Word."

"Fine."

"So... it's the first day of freshman year, and I'm sure you all remember how terrified you felt, especially after the Hall and all that bullshit. I was still pretty quiet at the time, and I walked into my first period English class composed of upperclassmen and a few scholar freshmen."

"Nerd alert!" Mars blurts.

"Shut up... what did I say?"

"Geez... fine... okay... okay."

"Anyways... there's only a few freshmen in the class and they're all up front, so I walk down the second aisle, sit down in the third row, look around, and see to my right that Vivian was sitting next to me... no big deal, right? The teacher had written a prompt on the board to get the lesson started. Everything was normal. The room was silent except for a few scribbles of mechanical pencils, and it's then that I noticed Vivian to my right begin to cover her nose as if she's about to sneeze. She did one of those silent sneezes that's awful, but way less embarrassing than a solid, A-CHEW. I followed with a subtle, "Bless you." Again nothing weird. Until it came again. I saw her rubbing her nose frantically, desperately, trying to hold it in. She sneezed again."

Knowing the next part, I can't stop myself. I laugh a little.

Curly jumps in, "That's it... she sneezed twice... mine come in threes."

"No… just wait… Once she finally lets go of the sneeze another sound comes out. *Poot!* Her entire face went."

Irish pulls my shoulder down. "Whoa… whoa… whoa… you're kidding me… Vivian Sneeze-Farted?"

"That's right, my man… Vivian Steele snarted."

Irish blows up in a cackle. He snorts out-of-control and it's contagious. Catching my breath and wiping a few tears, I say "Wait! There's more. After her face turned beet-red, she cowered at the table in horror praying to her paper that no one heard. She gathered a hint of courage, and looked around the room in desperation. The class was quite polite, there wasn't a reaction, until she looked in my direction. I was in such shock that I didn't even notice my finger was pointed at her with my jaw dropped. That's when I first saw the fury of Vivian Steele."

Irish speaks again, "So not only did she snart, but you pointed at her?"

"Yup… I didn't mean to. That's probably why she's hated me for so long."

Their laughter echoes through the Hill. This is one of the best parts of being a Jester.

Irish speaks one more time. "Ha, my man J. That made my day… cheers."

I'm about to take a swig when a blinding light shoots me. The Hill becomes glittered with red and blue lights—Berries. A shadowy figure points a gun at me and screams, "Put your hands up! Don't Move!"

Shit.

I drop the bottle and raise my left hand. I try to shade my eyes with my right, but the Berries shout even louder at the movement.

"What'd I say? Move again and I'll shoot that hand off!"

I count three figures in the dark. A bead of sweat streams down my forehead and drips off my eyebrow.

"What's your name?" a Berry commands.

Dammit. Dammit. Shit. I'm screwed.

They approach.

"Smoking, drinking, and God knows what," one of the officers says.

Another says, "Seriously, Curly, isn't this your third strike?"

His handcuffs clink.

Curly puts his head down and walks forward with his hands behind his back.

Before I respond, a breeze from behind me halts. Irish's bear-paw pats my shoulder.

One of the Berries looks at us and whispers, "Shit, it's him. The kid that saved Captain and his family from the crash."

Irish steps forward and towers over the police officer.

"What seems to be the problem, Officer?"

"It's McCook. And you know that, Irish."

Irish replies, "All Berries are the same. Cherries from across the Dam. Let's get it over with."

The officer with the cuffs jacks Irish in the back with a baton so the wounds won't show. Irish's expression remains dead. I try to help, but Irish raises his hand, and the Brigade holds me back.

The strikes to his back thump through the Hill. Because he doesn't wince or show any signs of struggle, the Berries hit him harder until he breaks down to all-fours. Next, they kick Irish's ribs. They stand him up and bombard his stomach with fists. Irish curls over. We watch helpless as our friend accepts a beating for us.

They finish with him, get in their car, and drive away.

Irish remains glued to their every movement and the Hill returns to moonlight. He yells, "Come on out, ya pansies. Actin' like you never seen a Berry before."

Mars crawls up from behind. He pats me on the back and says, "Berries are sketch."

Curly follows up with, "Yeah man, wicked buzz-kill."

I say, "You weren't the one that had guns pointed at you. I almost wet my pants. Thanks, Irish, appreciate it."

Irish winces and pukes on the ground. He wipes his mouth and limps towards us. Just before he falls over, we pick him up by the shoulders. Irish says, "Thanks mates. You know I would never let something happen to my loyal Brigade. There's nothing better than the rush of telling Berries to go back to hell. You guys up for another round?"

"Actually, man, I've had too much excitement for the day. I promised my mom I wouldn't be out too late," I say.

On the way home, Irish tells the story of the time he rescued the Captain from a car wreck. One I hadn't heard. Captain had been drinking and drove into a concrete wall. His patrol car caught on fire. Irish got him out there.

Irish attempts to light his own cig stick but his aching shoulders force him to drop it. I pick it up and light it for him.

"Thanks," he says.

We pull up to my house. The lights are off. I'm relieved that I can just head straight upstairs without talking to Mom.

Before exiting the limo, he asks, "Crazy first week, huh?"

"Ha, yeah. You're telling me. I'm just glad it's Friday. I'm gonna sleep all day tomorrow."

He puts his hand out for a quick shake.

"For sure, man. Me too. Hit me up tomorrow."

"Word."

I get out of the car, head straight to my room, and without a thought, I pass out.

6.

ROSE

POWDER MATCH: 55 DAYS

DOOBY BITES MY TOES the next morning. I take my shots of whiskey. Yesterday may have been some kind of crazy dream, until I realize I'm still wearing the same clothes. I wait as long as I can to leave my bed until the smell of freshly made toast makes my stomach growl. I take my slippers off, get out of bed, and catch a glimpse out of my window. My neighbor's shades are drawn.

It must have been a slow Friday night.

I go to my closet to get a robe. Out of the corner of my eye, I notice my neighbor watering a dead bush. It's like watching a refrigerator take a piss. Nice to see him doing something, I guess.

Why is he so familiar?

I walk down the stairs. Mom is drinking her morning glass of wine while eating jam and toast, continuing to work on the puzzle.

"Morning, Sweetie."

"Morning, Ma."

"Wow, you slept in late. Crazy night?"

"Nothing out of the normal. Just hung up at the Hill."

"You may need to find a new place to hang out. They're starting to develop over there now. More houses. More Berries."

It's almost like she knows what happened, but I'm so hungry, I don't think much of it.

"Yeah, it's getting weird up there; actually kinda creepy. Like a mansion graveyard."

"Well, just be careful, Sweetie. Don't want to lose the one and only man in my life."

She uses a brush to uncurl knots from her dry hair. She looks in the mirror, clipping her earrings. Beneath all that alcohol and weariness, there's still some lingering beauty.

"Okay, Ma."

She says, "There's toast and bacon on the table. Should be some leftover orange juice in the fridge."

"Thanks."

"Oh, J., I have to work this afternoon and probably late into the night, so you're going to have to fend for yourself for dinner."

"Work? On a Saturday?"

With a heavy sigh, she responds, "When do teachers ever stop working? I just have to set up some extra stuff in my classroom for the kids on Monday. Kathy is coming by, so you can take the truck."

"That's right. I forgot they changed the schedule this year. You start a little later. You excited to be the new fifth-grade teacher?" I ask.

She takes a deep breath and drinks some wine before coming out with it.

"Sure. I mean, every new year is exciting. I'm still going to miss being with the babies."

"Well, they need their best to get those kids ready for the new state tests, right?"

She takes a sip.

Mom used to be the best teacher in town. I can barely remember my teachers from last year, and don't even get me started with middle school. But for some reason, I can remember every teacher I had when I was in elementary. Those were the good days.

I give her a kiss on the cheek. The kiss is sour. I taste wine seeping through her pores. I head to the kitchen, and after a few bites, I look to the clock and can't believe it's already noon. After cleaning up the kitchen, I head back upstairs.

I open a can of beer from the tiny fridge next to my bed. I turn on the computer and check to see if anybody left me a message. Of course there's a police brutality video from Curly with the subject line: "Have A Berry Nice Day!"

I figure it's about time to do something with my life; a shower would be a good start. I head to the closet for a towel. Out of the corner of my eye, I see my neighbor watering the flowers. It's not strange that he's still watering the flowers, some people spend their whole day working in their yard. What's strange is that it's the exact same patch. He hasn't moved in what has to have been a half hour. A puddle is literally forming around his ankles and he isn't moving. I'm about to open the window and scream something at him until I see my neighbor's daughter.

So this is the girl that caused so much commotion in the Hall. I don't get it.

She comes from the front of the house with a cooler filled with beer.

Okay... that's pretty cool.

She opens a beer for him, places it in his right hand, makes sure he takes a drink, and like magic, he moves the hose to other parts of the garden. It's like she's his own personal bartender.

He pounds six beers one after another, non-stop.

Impressive.

She reaches on her toes to kiss him on the cheek and that's when she catches me.

I don't know what the hell made her look up, but our eyes make direct contact and instead of playing it cool, I jolt backwards in the most sketch manner possible. I don't even want to look back. She could just be waiting, then it would be a total shit storm. I decide not to look. The doorbell rings. My mom yells out, "Hey! J.! Sweetie! I'm headed out, but looks like there's a lovely girl at the door for you!"

Shit.

"Ma! Tell her I'm busy."

"Jester! Don't be rude! Put some clothes on! She's on her way up!"

Dammit, Mom.

I run to my room. I slip and jam my toe on the corner of my bed. I'd be cool with dying right now for sure. I try not to scream, fall over, and pick a piece of clothing off the floor when I hear the door crack open.

The only t-shirt I find is a gag-gift from Curly; a hot pink shirt with the acronym, T.W.A.T., standing for The War Against Terror.

A sweet voice comes from the other side of the bed.

"Hello? Is anybody there? It's Rose. Your neighbor."

Her voice is soft, delicate, warm.

"Umm, yeah sorry, I just stubbed my toe. I'll be a second."

The only shorts I find are a pair of old swim trunks from when I was a kid. They look like strawberry-colored short shorts.

I creep up from below my bed and see her standing there, a smirk creasing her pretty face. She tries not to laugh. Now that I see her up close, her black hair and long dark eye lashes frame her diamond-blue eyes so much that they sparkle. She must have been trying to hide her body at school yesterday because she has the curves of a vintage life-guard. She's wearing a creamy shirt that's too short to reach the seam of her black yoga pants. The right side of her lower stomach shows a tattoo of rainbow clovers.

"Sorry. Hi. I'm Jester. You can call me J."

I limp over to her side of the bed and reach out for a handshake.

"Can I shut the door?" she asks.

For the first time in my life, I'm speechless. My only thought is this exact situation happening in a vintage porno Irish and I saw. But that doesn't happen in real life.

"Sure. Go ahead."

She closes the door and I hear the click. She lets go of the knob and turns towards me, dragging her finger along my navy blue comforter. She picks up a picture of my parents smiling at the Bridge. She notices an old pile of magazines by my computer, and she sifts through every title.

"Old *Playboy* huh?"

I dart toward the mags and grab them from her hands.

"Good articles. Sorry. They're my friends."

She taps the keys on the computer. It wakes up to a title of my favorite book. *The Great Gatsby*.

"Good book," Rose says.

"Yeah."

She meets me face to face. Our noses are inches from each other. Her hair smells like sweet candy. Dreaming what's about to happen, I get so lost that I miss her fist curling into a brick.

SMACK!

She knocks me across the face... cold and hard. I'm nearly out. Next thing I know she's pressing both of her knees into my arms, pinning me to the bed, pinching the muscles in my jaw with her left hand and threatening me with the hard-as-brick fist on her right. Adrenaline takes over and even though she has a pretty good hold, I throw her off.

"Jesus Christ, girl! What the hell was that for?"

She raises her fist.

"Keep your eyes to yourself, you goddamn creeper."

"Okay. Whatever the hell you want. Just don't hit me again."

She glares.

"Good. Whatever you see or think you see, keep it to yourself, understand me?"

Leaning up on the side of my bed, she straightens her hair, pulls up a bra strap and stretches her clothes to look normal again. Even though my jaw hurts like shit, I regain enough composure to respond.

"I don't even know what you're talking about. So you gave your dad a six-pack, big deal. This is Ashton. More liquor here than water. My mom goes through a bottle of wine a day, and she's one of the better people in town."

She turns back and brushes a lock of hair from her eye.

"Really?"

"Yeah. Trust me. The people in Ashton are of two types. One is, they're Irish. Years ago many came down from Butte, Montana, to work the mines. And two, being Irish, they drink a hell of a lot of booze. From the look of it, your family will fit in just fine."

A smirk almost appears, but she stops herself.

"Didn't seem to fit in yesterday. What kind of psycho-bin of a school do we go to?"

Trust me. I hate it too.

"Yeah. Sorry about that. It's kind of a Vivian's tradition to pick kids for the Powder Match. There's a lot of people who would wish to see it die, even Irish himself, but Vivian has all the power with her dad running the factory in town, so what she says goes."

"Powder Match?"

"A competition with the Cherries. Vivian competes in the Chute, I'm Academia, and Irish is for the Snow Brawl."

"Irish? You mean that big, mafia-looking guy?

"Ha. I guess so. I never really thought about him like that, but yeah."

She cracks her knuckles one by one, thinking.

"So, he kind of rules everything?"

"Well, I don't know about *everything*. The answer to that question would need a book. But yeah, in simple terms, he does have a lot of power."

"And they call you Jester. So, you're what? Like his little puppet?"

Now I don't mind being nice to this girl, but that line pisses me off.

"I'm not his puppet. It's just easier to have a speaker. It makes things a little less personal. It's hard to explain."

"Less personal? Like *The Great Gatsby*?"

Her remark catches me by surprise.

"What do you mean?"

"You're his Nick Carraway."

I kind of hate the analogy because I think Nick Carraway is a total wuss, but I get the comparison.

"Yeah, in a way that makes sense."

"Okay. Why does he need it to be less personal?"

Most of her questions are pretty easy to give a vague answer to without really giving much up, but I don't trust her enough for that information. I take a few seconds to think about how to respond and read her. She's next to me, but she's not here. She looks around my room, analyzing music posters, and kicks some clothes from the floor. Maybe I could trust a girl that's crazy enough to come to my room and knock me down in order to protect her family.

"Look, it's honestly hard to explain. It's better to show you. How about this? I keep my mouth shut about your dad and you don't share with anyone what I'm about to show you. Deal?"

She mulls it over, but then she takes out her hand to shake mine.

"You have to drive though."

"Why?"

I'm a little buzzed.

"Don't ask."

"Deal."

"Okay, come with me." I take her hand to leave the room, but I get a glimpse on my door-mirror of what I'm wearing. "Let me change first?"

"Sure."

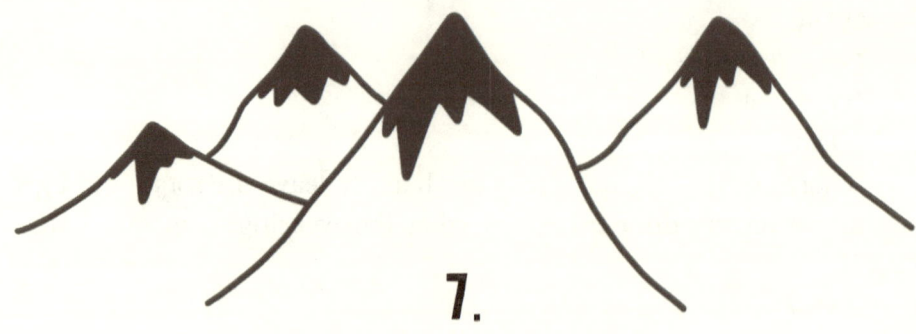

7.

ROAD TRIP

Rose drives Mom's rusted, red truck. I give her a brief tour of the town and explain about the games, but there's not much to see. Other than people passed out in gutters, we see a few broken down pubs and crumbling project-housing developments.

"So what's this you're showing me? And why is it so important?" she asks.

We leave the only real neighborhood in Ashton, The Hills at Ashton Creek. A few of the Activities Hall kids live up here. Christi, thank god for her family. They're normal. Although they only get a weekly shower like the rest of us, they at least eat dinner and stuff. Vivian's family would find a way to ruin this place if it weren't for the Dayes.

We drive through Five-Points. You'd think Rose would be terrified about cruising through a sketch part of town, but her eyes grow in curiosity. We circle a few hills and begin to climb the pass for a few miles until reaching a dirt road that slides down into the woods.

"So, about Irish," I say.

The road turns from dirt to gravel when we approach. It's hard to see due to the dust kicked up by recent visitors. Rose parks along the ridge and turn the ignition off.

"What is this place?" she asks.

"You'll see."

I open the glove box. A fluffy white polar bear Irish gave me rolls into my hands, and I put it into her lap.

She looks at it and asks, "What's this for?"

"How much does a polar bear weigh?"

She looks at me like I'm an idiot and says, "Um, I don't know, how much?"

"Enough to break the ice."

She rolls her eyes and says, "That was the lamest thing I've ever heard. Some Jester. No, but seriously, what's this for?"

"It's Irish's. Well, it's both of ours. We were in the hospital together during the holidays last year and he gave it to me. It was the only gift he could afford from the gift shop. It was the only gift either of us got for Christmas. And since the first time is different for everyone, I find it best you hold onto something."

She looks into its eyes brushing the back of its head with her thumb. I reach for the keys expecting her to back out, but she grabs my wrist and says, "Show me."

We head down a trampled path that swerves through walls of new-growth aspen and beetle-killed pines. She holds the bear in hand. A few hundred feet down from the lot, the forest opens to a space the size of a classroom. The flat ground is crusted dirt and pine needles. Guiding her arm with an open palm, I direct her to a couple of tree stumps where we sit. I pull out a flask and a pack of cig sticks.

"Want one?"

"One of what?"

"Um, a smoke? A swig? Anything?"

She looks at the flask.

"No, thanks. The bear is fine."

We sit in silence for the entire smoke.

"Look! If this is some pathetic attempt to get into my pants, then you can go…"

CRACK! BOOM!

She jumps toward me, holding the inside of my arm.

"Holy shit! What the hell is that?"

Her skin turns pale as she hyperventilates. She cradles the bear to her chest.

"Ha… just fine with the bear, huh? Don't worry, you'll be fine. It's just him."

"Him?"

I point to a patch of aspen trees in front of us.

"Yeah, Irish. He's over there. Take a look."

"You're not going to come with me?"

"You're walking ten feet. Just look down the hill. He's pretty hard to miss."

She takes a few steps and turns back to me. I wave the back of my hand to tip her in the right direction. She turns around holding the bear to her chest, and creeps to the trees as if going to witness a murder.

CRACK! BOOM!

Her shoulders cringe at the sound, but she continues.

I light up another cig stick and wait. When she reaches the ridge she drops the bear from her chest. She leans against the smooth bark of a tree and holds it, fascinated. She doesn't move. Even though Irish is a few hundred yards away, his size makes him look much closer. With a half-full gallon of water and an ax made for giants, Irish blasts at the trunk of a forty-foot tree behind his cabin. He takes a swig of the water, hits the tree one more time, and it cracks as it leans over. He pushes it down to steer the falling tree from his house.

"See, I told you, you didn't have to worry about anything."

She ignores me.

"What's he doing?"

"Well, he's cutting down trees."

"Screw you. You know what I mean."

"How else do you think he gets money?"

"He sells wood?"

"Amongst other things. He chops the tress as exercise to get stronger."

"He reminds me of someone I used to know. What do mean by get stronger?"

I show her a video of last year's Snow Brawl on my phone. It only takes a couple of minutes, but the highlights show numerous Cherries pummeling kids from Ashton on an open field. A leaderless Brigade, Mars, Curly, Twitch, and I try our best, but the Cherries bury us without Irish. Sonny almost kills Twitch with countless blows to his head. The video finishes with my jaw being broken by a blow from Sonny.

"Jesus, are you okay? Is that how you got that scar?" Rose asks.

I run my fingers along the ridges of the layered skin on my cheek.

"I'm alright. I was expecting a whipping. It hurt like shit, but the embarrassment from the annihilation was awful. I got away. Twitch got the worst of it."

"Twitch?"

"He's Irish's stepbrother. He is a genius when it comes to art. He and I won a couple of the Academia trials. Because Irish was in the hospital, Sonny took that as an opportunity to take down any chance of us winning Academia this year by eliminating Twitch on the Snow Brawl pitch.

"We almost won last year. The Snow Brawl in the next couple months is our last chance. We're both Seniors. Ashton needs the money for new pipes, drainage systems, or clean gutters. Anything that can get us water. We're tired of The Cherries taking all of our Sweets. We're tired of begging for employment from Vivian's dad. If we don't win, the Cherries are going to buy us out, and we're out in the desert with the rest of the world. I mean it's cold up here, but it's much better than the desert outside the mountains. Somehow, Irish finds a way to bottle and sell water. He's a man that can get things. He's been fighting as our Irish… for six years now. He's just now big enough that we may have a chance against Sonny."

"Sonny?"

"Sonny is the King of the Cherries. The big kid breaking me in the Snow Brawl. He's even bigger than last year. He over-medicates with our Sweets to grow."

"Six years? Irish has been fighting since he was twelve?"

"Yeah, he's pretty amazing considering you can die in the Snow Brawl. We need to listen to Vivian because she's the only person with money enough to get in Snowdrop Resort. So, she wins, for sure. And I'm all we have for Academia, so we lose by sheer numbers. But the worst part is getting our asses kicked in the Snow Brawl every year."

"So… he's been fighting for Ashton since the seventh grade?" she asks.

"Sixth. He's preparing for Sonny."

She looks back at Irish.

"He does this all for Ashton?"

"He was much different before his mother died. Mickey was different too. Back then Irish was talkative, excited, even hilarious at times. Ever since then, he's been a stoic, dedicated leader of the town. Ashton isn't a good place, Rose. You're lucky to get a good memory now and then, but the hardest part is dealing with the bad ones. I guess that's his way of dealing with it."

"So why do people come here?"

"Well, I think everyone has their own reason, but it's nice to know that our leader deals with similar demons."

"Demons? What do you mean?"

A slurred voice blares through the forest.

"Where the hell are you, Reginald? Get over here now!"

"Rose, we should go."

"No! I want to stay."

"I don't think you should see this."

I grab her hand off the tree, but she tears it away and looks back.

Irish's father, Mickey, steps into view. He stumbles with a bottle of vodka in one hand and a wrench in the other. His face is the color of a plum. This must be his sick way of training Irish. We can't hear anything, but he points at Irish with his bottle of liquor in hand. Irish just stands and looks at the ground without emotion. It doesn't take a second. The wrench whips across his face. Blood drips from Irish's mouth. He falls to the ground. His father starts on his back. Rose winces, about to scream, but I'm able to cover her mouth. She shivers in my arms, and I feel her clutching the bear in fear.

"Come with me. It's okay. Just come with me," I say.

I put my arm around her shoulder and lead her up the hill. We get in the truck. In shock, she sways back and forth. Rose turns the truck on, blasts the heat on full throttle, and waits until her breathing slows.

"I'm sorry you had to see that," I say.

"I want to go home," she replies.

She doesn't say a word the entire trip back. I don't blame her. Not many people have had to witness that.

She pulls into her driveway and turns the engine off. I expect her to run but she doesn't move. She sits frozen. I want to say something. She pulls the bear from her chest and hands it to me. With the sweet voice I heard from earlier this morning she says, "Thank you."

I give it back.

"Take her. She's yours," I say.

"I couldn't—"

I interrupt. "Don't worry about it. It's hard to find something nice here. Welcome to Ashton, Rose."

A tear drops from her eye.

"Thanks."

She begins to leave, but stops and turns around.

"You know, I'm not exactly new to Ashton," she says.

"What do you mean?" I ask.

"I was here for a little bit when I was younger. It's a long story, but I understand what you mean by bad memories."

"Oh, yeah?"

She turns to face me. "Yeah. Maybe I'll tell you sometime. But I only have one question."

"What's that?"

"Why did Irish follow me all the way through the hall yesterday?"

"You knew we followed you?" I ask.

"Well, yeah. Wouldn't you notice if Moses was parting the Red Sea behind you?"

"Ha, I guess so. I don't really know. I'm his best fri—, well, closest person he knows."

"Really?" She looks down at the bear and looks back to her house. "Well, thanks anyways for being so nice."

"Don't worry about it."

She leaves the car.

"Hey! Wait up a second."

"Yeah."

"Look, I know you want to keep your family stuff in-house, but on Sundays a few kids go to this thing called Al-Anon. It's for families dealing with alcoholics."

"Screw off!"

51

"No, wait! I mean, Irish is kind of forced to go. I go with him. You don't have to speak or anything. It's just an offer. It's at the Community Center in town. Sundays at seven."

"I'll think about it."

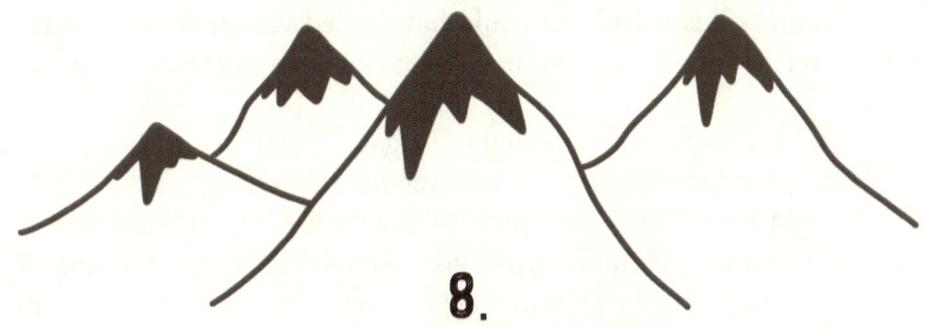

8.

THE MEETING

POWDER MATCH: 54 DAYS

IT'S SUNDAY EVENING. Irish and I sit in the limo. He takes a gulp of salt water, and spits it out with a bronchitis-like cough. I hear a gur-gled ball of mucus jump from his lungs into his mouth. He grabs an empty beer can from the floor of the truck and drips the clump from his mouth into the hole.

Gross.

After placing the can into the cup holder, he leans forward. The flame from his ancient lighter spotlights his face while he lights a cig stick. That's when I see it. His face. But it isn't *his* face. It looks as if someone had beaten a heart with a hammer. Covered with six-inch whip scars, his eyes are plum red. Those are a gift in comparison to the burn blisters covering his cheek. I've seen him after a beating many times before, we've all experienced a lashing, but this is something dif-ferent. His lacerations are still bleeding.

"What the hell? We got to get you to the hospital!"

His eyes turn to me.

"We're not going to do anything. A hospital will just report the abuse, and I'm not going anywhere."

"C'mon… this is bad. He could have killed you. It doesn't matter if he's a former Smoke Quartermate. He's not your *real* father. This has to stop."

He takes another swig and lights a cigarette with a mocking guff.

"Just get me to the meeting. Take me to the meeting!"

A slight buzz from a few pulls of my flask is the only thing that makes recounting certain memories tolerable. After six months of weekly meetings, Irish still hasn't said a word. After Mickey's wife died, Child Services said these meetings would be helpful for a healthy transition. I think it makes it worse. Especially with our new counselor.

As we arrive, Benny turns the engine off, but stays in the limo. Irish and I grab a few extra bottles of water, hustle to the building, and storm through the door. The counselor meets us, arms crossed wearing a black pantsuit with a white blouse. On the first day she was pretty, with a baby face, dimples, and flowing blonde hair. She couldn't be more than a year out of college. Now, pulled in a bun with a few dozen strands spread about, her hair is dry and lifeless. She used to let us call her Beth, but now it's Ms. McKeene.

McKeene calls us in.

Irish heads straight to the circle and places water on the floor for fellow kids.

"How are you, Jester?" she asks.

"I'm well, Ms. McKeene. Thanks for asking. Irish has had a rough day. I promise you he's glad to be here."

Her left eye gives a sketch squint like she knows I'm lying.

I look around the room to see if Rose has decided to attend. There's only one girl and it's not her. I know chances were slim, but her absence still stings.

Everyone meanders to a circle of chairs set for twenty guests, but only eight kids sit.

McKeene forces a conversation with the group by asking about our week and pressing a discussion of any current events. She's met with apathetic silence.

She rolls her eyes to the ceiling and gives a hopeless sigh. Looking to Irish she asks, "How about your family, Irish?"

Knowing she can't do anything to him, Irish sits hunched over his chair with his hood covering his face, showing only the bridge of his nose. He rests his elbows on both knees and rolls a lit cig stick, making the smoke dance through the fingers of his right hand. He takes another drag, leans back into a slouch with his face still cloaked. The stick rests low on his bottom lip. The room is silent as he takes three long drags. As it's about to die out, he pinches the filter, pulls it from his mouth, takes one last puff, and places the butt in his cantine.

I wish I could jack him across the face and say, "Stop being such a prick!" How hard is it to say, "No thanks, I appreciate the concern"? Instead, he decides to be a heinous silent dick.

I jump in and say, "My mom seems to be getting better."

McKeene's face lightens.

"Really? That's great, Jester! Would you like to share? I know we would all love to hear some good news."

I can tell from the dregs of conversation around the room that she's the only one listening. Plus, Mom's glass of wine is like drinking Kool-Aid compared to the liquor-soaked nightmares in this room, so I figure I'd help her a little.

"Well, I was worried she would drink more when they moved her to teach fifth grade. But she took up solving puzzles and has handled it well so far."

Her eyes open in hope.

"That's great! So, your Mom turned to a hobby to battle the stress instead of drinking. Good for her. Maybe we could all learn from Jester's experience."

I could interject and say she's *still* drinking while puzzling, but I allow the moment.

She asks the group, "So, does anyone know of your family members' hobbies?"

Not a moment after she finishes her question, a force of cold air and flurries of snow blow through the room in a wicked breath. The door clicks and clouds disappear. It's Rose.

Her jacket is so puffy, she's a walking pillow strangled by a scarf. With two black mittens, she holds Irish's polar bear. The room is still as she places the bear in an empty seat next to her. It takes an effort for her to remove her winter clothing. Slight sparkles of glitter scatter through her hair and eyelashes. She places her coat and scarf on the back of the chair. Her cheeks are flush, illuminating her eyes. Turning to McKeene, she says, "Sorry I'm late, Miss. I'm Rose. I had a little trouble getting here."

She looks at me and then at Irish before saying, "I was invited by a few friends here. I hope it's okay if I can sit in."

"Have a seat."

"Thanks."

"Jester was just about to continue."

Rose isn't afraid of him like everyone else. She sits down, crosses her legs, and stares right at him.

Irish stares at the bear. They don't move.

As I'm about to begin, he bursts from his chair and leaves the room. I follow him, failing at multiple attempts to grasp his shoulder. I get a good grip, and he turns with the same raging eyes from a few days ago.

Meanwhile, McKeene calls for a break.

Irish is in a rage. "What the hell do you want, Jester?"

"Nothing. I'm just saying—"

"Just saying what?"

"Will you just go back? I invited her."

"You did?"

"I've told you about her dad. He drinks. Figure it could help."

"You know, J., sometimes it's best you don't know everything."

He presses my shoulder with his hand to move.

What don't I know?

Back in the room, the air is tight. Each kid is leaning over their chair, wide-eyed and in shock. The room is stone. Rose is the only one looking away. She sits cross-legged, while cracking each finger.

He and I have been to countless meetings. This is the first time he speaks. McKeene is so shocked she ignores his lighting another cig stick.

Irish coughs twice, blows a cloud to the light above, and speaks in short bursts like a cracked faucet. He is now the center of attention.

"Six years ago when I was twelve or so, my dad, Mickey, was always over at Jimmy's house. He wouldn't give a shit about me. He didn't care if I ever went to school. He sure didn't care if I smoked. At Jimmy's house, it sucked getting matches, and a bitch to get cig sticks. I had to dig through his ashtrays for unfinished butts. Jimmy always left his lighter on the front porch, so I took it."

Irish has Jimmy's lighter?

Irish flicks his lighter and continues. "I lit a cig stick up, had a few puffs, and that's when I threw the butt in the dry bush next to Jimmy's house. In seconds, I saw the smoke making its way through Jimmy's house. I tried to get water. We just didn't have enough. I'll never have enough."

It was him? Irish started the fire? I thought Jimmy did.

I glance at Rose. Now her eyes are on him. Irish coughs.

"I ran as fast as I could. But there just wasn't enough water."

Irish presses the embers in his calloused hand and tosses the dead butt on the floor. He lights another.

"Smoke poured through every crack of the house. Once I opened the door my skin felt boiled from the heat."

Tension fills the room when Irish leans forward and laughs to himself, while playing with the smoke between his fingers. He sniffs and coughs a little.

"I saw Jimmy and Mickey passed out on the floor. I dragged them out of the house. Then I heard her screams. The worst of it were her screams."

Irish's body changes. He becomes tense, pulls his hood over, and begins to grind his hands.

"There's nothing worse than hearing a girl's tearful screams. I ran upstairs to her door and kicked it in."

Irish looks at Rose.

"When I kicked down the door, I saw a beautiful black-haired angel. I grabbed her and got out of there."

Irish blasts an empty chair across the room and continues.

The room screeches from pushed back chairs.

He cracks his knuckles. Rose looks at him.

Reaching for his pack, Irish's hands tremble as he searches the empty box. I light one for him and place it in his mouth. Irish continues to retell his nightmare.

"It was my fault. The fire was my fault. Jimmy took the fall for me. I never saw him again, and I never heard of his daughter again either. I never thought anything of it, until a few days ago. Until I saw her enter this room, just now. It's nice to meet you, Rose."

Damn. Rose's dad is Jimmy.

There isn't an eye off Irish. His eyes are on her. Her eyes on him. Gripping the scarf in her hand, she wipes away tears.

I'm speechless with the rest of the room. I look to Ms. McKeene. She's stone.

Rose pulls the chair, puts on her coat and scarf, and heads out the door without a word. I look back at Irish. I want to yell at him to run after her, but he hunches towards the ground. A tear crawls down the lumps of his blood-bruised face.

"I'm sorry," is the last thing I say.

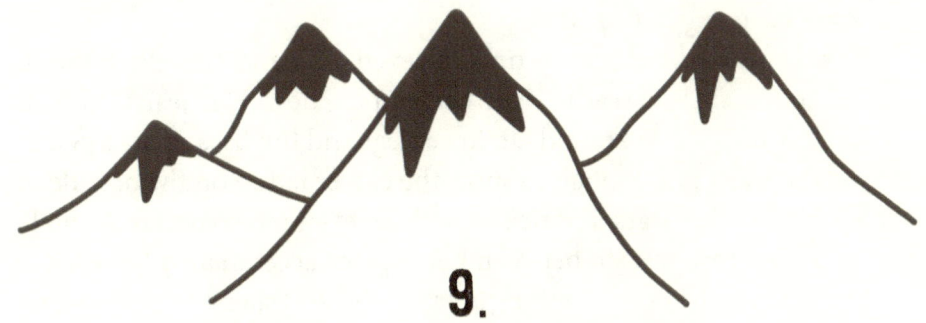

9.

BACK TO NORMAL

POWDER MATCH: 53 DAYS

IT'S MONDAY. Colored hoods move in waves along brick walls of the Hall. Mars's Quarter heightens the atmosphere with reverberating cackles. Underclass benches whisper in hidden conversations, while Vivian and her chicklets text and give conversational smirks shaming kids on the school bio-site. Irish's face is recovering, but still swollen from the beating. Most of his scabs are clean. A few remain covered in white tape over his cheek and eyebrows. He sits in silence ruling the Hall with brutish eyes.

I catch a glimpse of Christmas Daye in the middle of Mars's bench. She's glowing, showing no fear from Vivian's transaction. Her popping blue eyes and dimple-framed smile shine in laughter as if she's won a big prize. I'm happy for her, but it still hurts to see her on the other end of the Hall. Her eyes take a quick turn towards mine as if she knows I'm staring and we meet in a frozen moment. The moment melts when a single door opens and like a vacuum the Hall is empty. The only way to describe the moment I see her, is—fantastical. A gust of silence blows past each bench as if seeing Aphrodite. She's too far away at first to recognize, but after a few more steps, I know right away it's Rose. A sharper-looking Rose.

Vivian is going to be pissed.

Rose wears a black, body-tight, sleeved "T", and her glossy black hair of gentle curls cascades over her ample chest. Her jeans, torn in spots, show milky skin around her lower legs and thighs, and are low-cut around the waist just enough to show the clover tattoo on the outside of her left hip. As she nears, I notice something even more special. A small, sky-blue glass rose rests in between her breasts, accentuating her eyes.

She reaches the bench looking at Irish, still and silent. I turn towards him. Staring at the ground, he doesn't even know she's there.

I nudge him with my elbow. He doesn't move. I nudge him again. He doesn't move. I hit him.

He's ready to throw a fist at me when he notices the look on my face and my finger pointing towards her. He turns. An unlit cig stick drops from his mouth to the crotch of his pants.

Vivian and her Chicklets are too busy sucking at life to notice, until Rose's perfume wafts to our benches.

Vivian screeches, "Who's this slut?"

Rose shoots a threatening glare before she says, "Watch your words."

Vivian jumps up ready to pounce when Irish raises his hand. He stands up, locking his eyes on Rose. He towers over her by almost a foot. Her eyes gaze upward with long butterfly lashes. A few seconds pass before anything happens. The only sound is Viv's heavy breathing. I can smell the coffee on her breath.

Then, in a subtle, provocative motion, Rose brings her right arm forward. It's the bear I had given her yesterday.

She says, "I believe this is yours. I just wanted to say thank you for saving my father and me." Irish takes the bear from her hands. Seconds pass. He looks down at the bear and brushes its white fur. I don't know if he wants to speak or wants me to speak. Just before I'm about to talk, Rose takes over.

In a confident, mannered tone, she places her left palm out and asks, "You know… I'm still having a hard time finding my way around this place. Would you mind walking me to class?"

He takes her hand. With a smirk, he nods to me and walks alongside her to the Academic Hall. Not a moment after their feet leave the red brick, the bell rings for first period.

Shit. Well, if Irish wants Rose, Vivian is out. What are we going to do now?

For the first time in my life, I use school work to pass the time. But it isn't all bad. Ms. Madonna, the beauty from next door, is really an amazing teacher. I actually like drawing now.

The fourth period bell rings, and I head to Irish's limo for lunch at the Bridge. After waiting in anticipation, then frustration, Irish doesn't show. The doors open and it's—Mars. He nods to me and walks towards us.

"What's up, J? Where's Irish?"

"I don't know. You didn't see him in there?"

"Nah, I'm the last out. Maybe he's with that new girl of his."

"You think?"

"Maybe. No, he's never missed a midday drink at the Bridge. I wouldn't worry about it, man. He's probably just making up missed time with a teacher. You know that fool never goes to class. And if he does, he's always late."

"Yeah... I guess."

"Need a ride?"

"For sure man, thanks."

Mars's car is a dump. Some rusty old clunker from a couple decades ago. It takes him at least three or four tries to get the thing started and when it does, it almost explodes.

"You know, Mars, maybe Five-Points wouldn't attract so many Berries if you'd just let this thing die in peace."

He caresses the dash and says, "Not my baby; we're in love."

The power steering screeches from the lack of fluid. After a few jolts, we head towards the Bridge.

The Bridge is on the other side of Ashton. It takes a few minutes to get there, but something about the drive shines a light on reality. There's more to life than the Ashton trenches. The Bridge rests below the base of the Dam that extends to the other side of the valley. Getting there, we have to climb a steep hill, and at its peak the valley lights up from the tropical plants of Cherry Ridge. Its beauty stings every time we roll over.

The Steeles are the only family in Ashton that can afford the Snowdrop Resort. Damn Vivian uses it to her advantage. She's the only one who can practice the Chute. Hidden by the smoke of Ashton's Sugar Sweet factory, we don't exist to the outside world, and that's the way the Cherries want to keep it. We fall below the height of the Dam and approach the Bridge.

It's an old pub. I don't know if it's technically a pub. It's the size of a restaurant. But when we open the century-old, cracked, wooden door, the homey smell of smoke and liquor makes it feel like a pub. The walls are bordered by booths with cracked red leather lit by a low hanging light for all of the Quarters, with a few others left for regulars, or lost tourists.

We use Cherry profits from selling Sweets to pay off Seamus, an old Irishman from the homeland who runs the place.

Seamus is hard up for money, so he's forced to serve booze to minors. He pretty much offers you a stout or whiskey, unless you're a girl, then he may reach for other liquors in the back. He wouldn't give Vivian her martini if it weren't for Irish.

A cloud hovers over Curly's booth; Mars's is pretty loud taking shots. Even Christmas is smiling, starting to fit in. Vivian's booth is a teenage scene from hell. Conversations are held through cell phones. We approach Irish's booth in the far left corner. Curly is already sitting with an ashtray full of cigarettes, along with Shea. We sit down as Seamus sets a bottle of whiskey and fresh stouts of beer from the cask. He pours four shots for us, pours another for himself, and raises the glass in cheers. Slamming the shots, we each take a sip of beer and shake his hand with our weekly $50.

He says, "My thanks, mates."

We wait for him to walk away. Curly speaks up with a little curiosity and confusion.

"Hey man, where's Irish? What happened this morning? That was messed up." He points to a kid in his booth passed out with his head on the table and says, "Even my main man, Willie, talked about that shit, and he can barely tell the difference between dreams and reality."

It's about time someone else is worried about Vivian. She could bail on the Chute. Then what can we do?

After taking a quick glance around the room to see if anyone is possibly near, I lean into both of them. They lean in with me.

"Curly, I don't know where he is. I waited for ten minutes next to his limo and he never came out. Right, Mars?"

He gives an elbow to my arm and says, "It's true, Curly. J. was looking like a little kid who lost his mom at the mall."

Curly covers his mouth trying to hold back a laugh.

"Seriously, fellas, when has Irish ever missed a Bridge meet up… ever?"

Looking at each other and then back at me, they say, "Never."

"I know, right?"

Mars shoots a glance towards Vivian's booth and asks, "Not to mention, what about Vivian? Not that I don't care about Irish and all, but her family runs the housing in this town, and that new girl faced her hardcore in front of everyone."

Curly responds, "For sure, J. The majority of my business is with those rich assholes."

Mars says, "Vivian's dad is the only guy fighting off the Cherries from pushing the families in Five-Points out. What are we supposed to do after that?"

"Look, fellas, you think I don't know about this shit? I was going to talk to Irish on the way over here, but he didn't show up. Look, like you said, Mars, he probably just got held up with a teacher for missing class, and the girl thing is probably just him putting on a show or something."

They look at each other again while taking another sip of beer. Shea nudges Curly to look right and he coughs up some foam. Under his breath he says, "J., Vivian is headed over here, and she looks pissed."

"Just play it cool," I say.

I prepare for her wrath. I can tell she's right behind me by the flowery smell cascading from her. Curly tries to break the tension by saying, "Hey, Vivian. You look really pretty today. Is that a new perfume?"

"Screw off, Curly."

"Okay Mars, I think that's our cue."

They crawl out and go to their Quarter booths, but Shea stays silent, staring at her.

"It's okay, Shea. Why don't you have a drink with Seamus and the regulars. It'll just be a minute."

He leaves and she takes his spot.

"Where the hell is he?" Vivian asks.

I take a sip of beer.

Her tone is explosive. "Screw you, Jester! Where is he? If he's with that trick, I'm going to flip shit!"

"I don't know, Vivian. I honestly don't know."

I wince, expecting to get slapped.

"Who is she?"

"Who?"

She takes the beer out of my hand and follows with an impressive gulp. She wipes off some foam from her upper lip and plays with the glass with both hands like she's contemplating smashing it against my face.

She asks again, "The girl in the Hall today? Who is she?"

I don't know what to say.

She's just my next door neighbor. Oh! And there's a small tidbit about her being the daughter of Jimmy, the legendary Irish. The daughter that our Irish saved... psshh... yeah right.

"Vivian, I'm just as confused as you. All I know is that her name is Rose, and that she must be pretty smart being in the Academic hall. In all the years I've known Irish, he's never behaved like this. Especially when it comes to the matters of Ashton."

The front door creaks open and sunlight bursts in. We both look back in hope that it's him, but the shadowy figure haloed in bright light appears to be one of Curly's mates. Looking back to Vivian, I catch a tear trickling from her left eye. I sense her crushed spirit. With a slight sniffle, she says, "It's not supposed to be like this. This is my year. I earned it. I paid my dues. Why doesn't he want me?"

I can't believe I feel sorry for her.

I reach my hand to hers, which curls around the glass. "Vivian, I'm sure it's nothing. Irish is still yours. Everything will be fine."

I wait a few seconds in hope for her to respond, but she refuses to take her eyes off the glass. I lean in closer and dip my head trying to glance towards her eyes expecting to see pools forming. Instead, sweet Vivian disappears. She rips the glass from my hand and breaks it against the wall. She points at me and screams, "Screw you, Jester!

That's not a part of the deal. You tell him to get his shit in order, or my family is pulling the plug! Do you understand me? Figure it out, now."

She snaps at her booth and the girls gather behind her like ducks as she storms out. Silence fills the room. Seamus comes over to pick up the glass, but I stop him. "Don't worry, Seamus, I'll clean it up."

Mars and Curly give a quick whisper to their mates to reassure everything's cool, and as they come back to the booth with Shea, the room picks up to a steady volume.

Helping to pick up the glass, Mars speaks up. "Damn, dude, she's pissed as hell."

Curly follows after, scooping up the glass into a dustpan. "For sure, man, major buzzkill. What did you say?"

I can't hold back. "Nothing, Man!" Looking to Shea, I tap on his shoulder and say, "Go find him. He's got to be at school. Let me know right away."

Without a word, he gives a me bump of his hand and shoots out the door.

The fellas get back into the booth and call for another beer. Seamus drops them off, but I still can't control my mind from thinking about what to do.

Mars asks, "You all right, man? Irish always comes through."

"Yeah, I guess so. We need Vivian, though. And this new girl messed that shit up."

Mars responds, "True, true… Five-Points is happy to have Christmas, but rumors have spread. Five-Points is worried."

Curly jumps in. "I don't know, bruh. It's not that bad."

"What do you mean?"

He gives a look to Mars's booth and when I turn around Christi is staring right at me. Like an idiot, I look down like I was the one caught looking. I take a deep breath, glance up, and she gives me a shy smile. I grab the neck of my shirt and give a "that was sketch" look. She covers her mouth with a slight giggle and my body warms in sensation. I wish I could just focus on her. That would be the shit.

I don't know what scares me more, my feelings for Christi, or Irish's feelings for Rose.

Mars jumps in from behind. "Damn, dude. Christmas Daye? Go over and talk to her."

I look to him and say, "Yeah, right, man. Maybe one on one, but in front of Five-Points kids, that's social suicide."

"They're not that bad, dude. I can get them to bounce out if you want," Mars says.

"No. Just stop it. I'll figure it out on my own..."

I look back again and give her a smile when my phone vibrates.

Shea: **Found him. He's in the cafeteria. Want me to get him out?**

I look to the fellas and say, "Shea said, 'He's in the cafeteria.'"

Confused, they respond, "With the Nerds?"

"I guess so. And stop calling them Nerds. I'm a Nerd, you know... technically."

They roll their eyes. I get another text.

Shea: **He's with that girl. Respond A.S.A.P. Vivian walking up to the doors.**

I text back: **Get out! Now! I'll be there in a bit. Distract her. She can't find out Irish is with Rose.**

Shea: **Word.**

I tell Curly to stay and keep things calm, while Mars and I head back to school. Curly asks, "What are you gonna do?"

"I don't know, man. I'll figure something out."

10.

AN IRISH EXIT

IT TAKES LONGER THAN expected because Mars's car shakes at any speed above 35 MPH, but we reach the school and run to the doors. Just before we reach them, I hold Mars back to catch a breath and to try to act casual. We wait in the mid-way passage before the second set of doors, looking through the windows. The benches are cleared except for Vivian's. They're all focused on their phones, so we have a chance to sneak in. With both of us entering, two doors may be too much to notice. The only chance is if I follow Mars.

I hide behind the door to the left as he opens the one on the far right. Once they notice it's just him, their eyes creep back to their phones. He holds the door as long as possible, and I catch it just before it clicks to close. I slither through the crack of the door, crawl along the wall, and enter the cafeteria.

Massive windows bring life to the air in the cafeteria. It's pretty cool. Kids walk from table to table with smiles and laughs. Seniors sit with freshmen; sophomores with juniors.

I search around the room and see him.

I get a text from Shea: **Chirp coming for Vivian's latte.**

Irish is smiling. Rose sits across from him giggling and talking to the person next to her. I approach the table. Her eyes meet mine along with the rest of the table as I tap him on the shoulder. He turns around with a surprising shine to his face. He stands up, they follow, and he opens his palm.

"Uh… um… well hey, guys. Hey, Rose, nice to see you again."

Rose speaks up. "Hey, Jester, why don't you have a seat?"

I turn around, look back, and see Chirp grabbing Vivian's latte. I run to her before she can see Irish.

Chirp asks, "What are you doing in here, J.?"

She looks over my shoulders on her tiptoes and catches him with Rose.

"What the hell J.? Is that Irish with that girl?"

"What girl?"

"You know what girl I'm talking about."

"Chirp. You can't tell Vivian."

"But—"

"Chirp. I know you aren't happy. Look at Irish."

She looks behind me again and sees a different Irish.

I plead. "C'mon, please, Chirp. He's smiling."

"It doesn't matter, J. Vivian needs to win the Chute for us, and if she hears that Irish is with another girl… there's no way. Sorry, J."

I grab Chirp's arm as she turns to the Hall.

"And what's telling Vivian going to do, Chirp?"

She stops.

"You have to trust us. We'll figure something out. We always do," I say.

She turns around and says, "I have to get Vivian's latte," and walks down the cafeteria hall to the kitchen. I watch in hope and watch her as she exits. I head back to Irish.

I wouldn't mind sitting down and catching my breath, but I have to update him on the whole Vivian situation. It's the first time I've seen people not begging for water from Irish. I ask her, "Rose, I have to speak to Irish about something, if that's okay?"

She looks to him. He gives her a nod and signals for the rest of the table to sit back down. I pull him aside. He leans down as I whisper a recounting of the whole situation.

He looks up and rubs the stubble on his chin, considering his next move. He pats me on the shoulder, smiles, and looks towards the student kitchen workers.

Why is he smiling? This isn't a game.

The metal gates close, shutting down the kitchen. The smell of chicken noodle soup lingers, then escapes the air. The lines close down and one by one tables begin to clear. We wait until most of the room is empty. Kids around our table get up and throw out their trash. Irish walks around to grab Rose's tray and throws out the trash for her.

The cafeteria herds out. He crouches trying to avoid an inquisition from Vivian. He pulls me with him past the edge of the Hall. When we're in the clear, he holds my chest back to stay as he walks a few steps and whispers several words to Rose while holding her hand. He raises her to her tiptoes and she gives him a hug, then leaves. He watches her walk the entire way until she's out of our view. As he turns, a smile breaks the tape covering one of his scars. Before turning the corner with me, he whispers in my ear, "It's all good, man. I promise. Whatever you say, I'm here with ya. We'll get through this. It's just Vivian. Remember, the snarter… ha-ha."

I want to knock him out for putting me through all this shit. But it's nice seeing him a little happy.

"Fine, dude. I'll get us out of this shit. But we got to talk right after school about this mess."

He crunches his fist and our knuckles meet.

"For sure, man."

We turn the corner and Vivian is ready to pounce. We approach the bench. Her legs are crossed, with the foot on top tapping. She glares as if planning his murder. I'm only a few feet away, she shoots up, throwing her cell phone to the floor. Both her arms are straight at her sides with hands clenched, and I expect the beast from before, but nothing comes out. Without looking to her, Irish sits down next to her bench in his recliner and points for me to speak. I look to her, but her eyes are set towards him, eyebrows cinched tight.

"Irish wants to apologize for his absence today. He was in the library making up an assignment for missing his summer reading."

Her eyebrows unknot, but she still remains stiff and says, "And the girl? What about the girl? Let him speak for himself!"

"She's his neighbor," Irish says, "Part of Ashton like all of us."

I take a deep breath and say, "Look, again, she's my neighbor. She moved in a few days ago. She doesn't know anything about our world, and the very first day you treated her like a piece of shit. All the other kids know about the Hall. They know what to expect. She didn't. He just did what any Irish would do and welcomed her to the community. That's it."

Her lips grind. She relaxes and turns towards me. "Why didn't you say that earlier then?"

"First of all, Vivian, it's not my job to keep you informed. My job is to speak for Irish. Plus, I would be more inclined to help you if you weren't such a… you know. Besides, he just told me minutes ago."

She takes a step towards me, raising her nose to meet mine. She presses her finger to my chest and with quiet anger says, "You listen to me, you fool. I don't care what your job is. We have a deal. Either I get Irish, or find a new competitor for the Chute. If I don't get my way, Ashton will no longer exist in this valley. So, you better get your handsome Irish on board."

She finishes with a kiss on Irish's cheek and a quick slap saying, "See ya later, Irish baby." She blows him a kiss, flicks her hair, and leaves as her ducklings follow towards class.

See, Irish. She knows and is pissed.

I take a seat next to him and he places a hand on my shoulder to say thanks, but I can't take it. I throw it off and tell him, "Your limo. After school. This is serious shit."

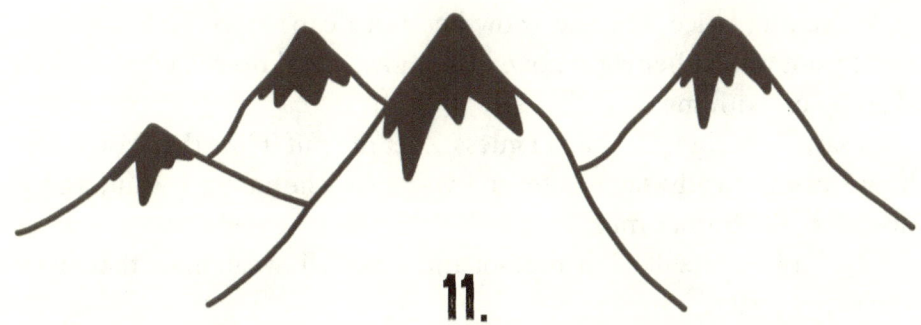

11.

RIDICULOUS AWESOMENESS

THE FINAL BELL RINGS and outside, I see Irish with the Brigade at his limo in the back of the parking lot. I walk up and I see him give each guy a slick five-spot and some extra water for the help at lunch. They give me a quick, "What's up?" and head out in their separate directions. Shea sticks around to see if any more help is needed, but Irish sends him away. Irish puts his hand out for a shake and takes me in for a hug to get in the limo. Benny drives.

Okay, J. How do we do this? Delicately…

We get in. I can't tell if I'm mad because he bailed without telling me, or that I'm a little jealous. Rose is beyond good-looking. I light up a cig stick and hand it to him. I light my own saying, "Sooooo… turns out Rose is hot as hell, ha-ha. Man, I didn't see that coming at all."

After exhaling, he puts both hands to his forehead and with a sigh of surprise says, "I know, man… she's… she's… she's just ridiculously awesome in every way."

"Ha… I didn't know 'ridiculously awesome' was in your vocabulary."

I gaze out the window.

"She must be a pretty cool girl," I say.

He turns on the music, looks in the mirror to check his face, and says, "You know, J. … it's not just that she's pretty. I don't know what it is. We've met twice. I barely know her and I can't stop thinking about her. I want to text her right now… and now… and now… what the hell is going on with me, man?"

I say, "Um… well… ha… I guess… let me put it like this. You know how I can basically say whatever I want, to whomever I want, and it doesn't really bother me?"

He looks at me like I'm an idiot and says, "Uh, yeah man, that's why you're my Jester."

"I know. But when I look, or am around, or even think about Christmas Daye, words don't even exist. It's like my heart shuts off my brain. Either that or it's coming from another body part."

He smacks my arm laughing, and says, "Christmas, really? I had no idea, man."

"Yeah… she's… she's *my* 'ridiculously awesome.'"

"Ha. Wow. Good for you, dude. I wish you would have said something. I wouldn't have accepted Vivian's trade to Mars's quarter."

"Don't worry about it. I kind of like that she's over there. She smiles a lot more now that she's not one of Vivian's Chicklets. Plus, you and I both know Five-Points is a blast. They may be the poorest part of this valley, but they sure know how to have a good time."

He pulls two fresh cans of sparkling water from behind the seat and hands one to me. After a few sips in silence, he asks, "So… is this… like… what love feels like?"

Holy shit. Irish just said the word, "Love." We're in trouble.

I almost spit out half my water and say, "What are you asking me for? I don't know. I think this is what they call 'crush mode.'"

He looks at his phone thinking.

Should I bring up all that Vivian stuff?

"'Crush mode,' huh?"

I hit the window and Benny stops the limo.

I ask, "What about Vivian?"

I know we have to deal with it and figure something out, but I like seeing Irish excited, talkative, showing moderate signs of personality. For the first time in our friendship, we actually get to be friends.

We pull up to my house and finish off the last few sips. The limo shuts down and he stares at Rose's house. "I can't believe you get to live right next to her. You're an ass. I bet she's up there reading some big book with those sexy reading glasses and in skimpy pajamas," he says.

"Whoa… whoa… easy, Irish. Leave those thoughts for your private time."

He looks at his phone strumming his thumbs and asks, "Hey J.?"

"Yeah?"

"You think you could help me come up with something to text her?"

"Sure, man. Give me your phone."

I text for him: **Hey Rose, What's up? Just wanted to say I had fun at lunch. How's your night going?**

"There you go, man. That's it. Press send and the rest is on you."

"Cool… Thanks, J."

"No worries, man. I'll see you tomorrow."

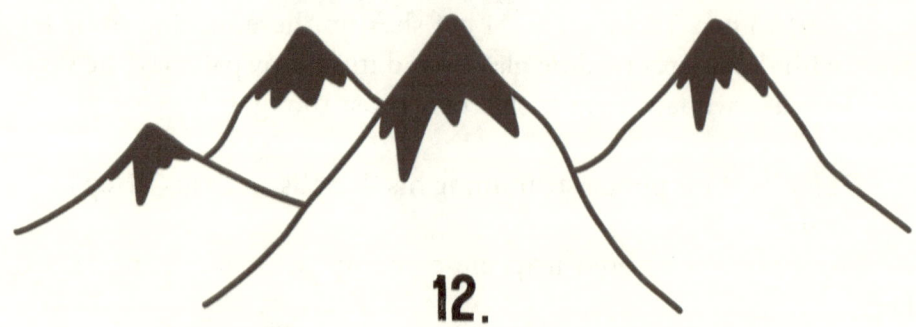

12.

STEAKS AND POTATOES

Dooby is barking. He never barks. I turn the key to my house and focus on the stairs and the warmth of my bed. But once I open the door, my hope is broken by the smell of fresh steak and buttery potatoes. The smell tells me to adjust my plans for one of Mom's PTSD episodes.

I walk through the door, look to the right, and three bottles of wine sit alone next to a completed puzzle of Powder Valley on the table. A creak of wood sounds and I hear her slurring her words. It's my mother.

"J., is that you!?"

My body reacts to the smell and my heart begins to beat out of control. Nausea builds. I try to control it by taking deep breaths, but my lungs shut down and I start to gag.

Panic attack.

Tears run. I hold back the sound of sickness to make sure she doesn't hear. I grasp the bannister of the stairs, close my nostrils, and fight to take several deep breaths through my mouth to settle my body.

"J., is that you?"

I fish the bottle of eye drops from my pocket, apply some into my eyes to relieve redness and respond, "Yes, Mom. It's me."

Jubilant, she says, "Jimmy's back in town! Come to the kitchen, Sweetie! I need your help before Dad gets home. He'll be here any minute. It's a surprise."

Shit. Everything got so cluttered, I forgot Jimmy could trigger one of Mom's episodes.

The delicious smell stings at each step. I walk to the kitchen and my stomach hurts. As I turn the corner, I see her. Standing over the stove, she sways with a glass of wine in her hand, wearing a skimpy red dress. She sings along with their wedding song, *I Will Always Love You.* Curls bounce to her shoulder as she sprinkles spices and seasoning onto the dishes. She looks like her old self. I fight to ask, "What's the special occasion, Mom?"

After taking a sip from the glass, she checks the bread in the oven, turns around, looks at me with glossy eyes, and scampers across the kitchen bare-footed, giving me a sloppy, minute-long hug. Still holding the glass, she lays her head on my shoulder, and with a slur she asks, "Did you see? I finished it. I finished the puzzle. I wanted to frame it for your dad. But I just couldn't wait. You think he'll like it?"

If he was alive.

Tears sting my eyes. To stop them, I blot my eyes out with my thumbs.

"Of course, Mom. He'll love it. But with one look at you, I don't think the puzzle even matters."

She pulls away and holds my shoulders. Her wine breath pours at me as she gazes at me saying, "How could we be so lucky to have a son like you? So sweet. So handsome. We've never been so proud. And your senior year, too." She releases one hand to finish the glass, places it on the table, and taps me on the shoulder saying, "Now, Sweetie, be a doll, get a glass from the cupboard and fill both up for when he gets home. I want everything to be perfect."

Turning around, she trips over her own ankles and stumbles, but grasps the counter to keep her balance. She tries to walk towards the stove. I hold her arms still to keep her stable.

She places the back of her hand to her forehead saying, "Whoa... Mommy's feeling a little dizzy."

I grit my teeth and say, "Hey Mom, Dad's going to love this. The puzzle is beautiful. You're beautiful. This food is beautiful. But I think it's time for you to relax. How about I finish things up in here, and we give him a big surprise together. What do you say?"

She turns around, places her hand on my cheek, and says, "Such a sweet boy."

I guide her to the couch and place the glass on the table. After setting the playlist to their list of wedding songs, I head to the kitchen to finish the meal. Finishing the meal is the *worst* part.

I look at the steak sizzle in the pan, and can't tell if my stomach growls from hunger or from pain. With the juices still bubbling, I hold it below my nose and inhale. The smell is rancid with disgust and despair.

I'm sorry, Dad. I'm sorry, Mom.

I cut a small piece of steak and feed it to Dooby. After breathing out, I hold the pan over the trash can, turn it over, and drop the steaks into the trash. Next, the mashed potatoes. Then, the bread. I take the garbage bag and put it in the garage.

I head into the living the room. Like the countless times before, Mom lies there like she's crashed through the roof, out cold. Dooby drags a blanket from upstairs. I brush a few stray strands of hair from her forehead. I push her to the side so that her chest faces the backside of the couch. Dooby climbs up to the end of the couch. One by one, I collect the puzzle in the box. I place the blanket over her and turn off the music. I turn off the lights. I turn off our former life.

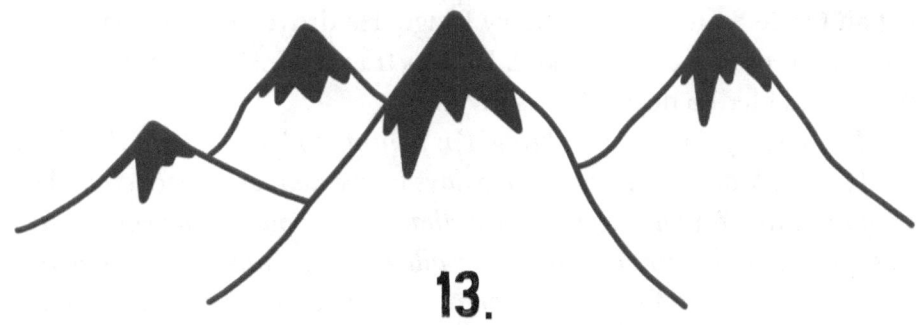

13.

DAD AND JIMMY

POWDER MATCH: 50 DAYS

I'VE NEVER BEEN AFRAID of the dark. The gloom welcomes me. Makes me feel safe. Like being cloaked in a warm blanket. I can turn off reality with the flick of a switch. I head to my room and towards the closet. I pull out an old shoe box and open the lid. The aroma of oil-soaked leather streams through my nose like a drug. Nothing smells quite like a baseball glove. Euphoria takes over. I pull out the glove my father gave me on his last day.

Surrounded by darkness, it's like he's still here. Strumming my fingers along the oiled leather, I don't need to see the message burned into the hide to know what it says.

"To the best son a father could ask for. You're the light of our little family. The light that burns away the dark. I love that you're my son. Keep burning bright and take this town out of its ashes."

A tear trickles into the corner of my mouth while another drips on the leather.

Dad died in a car crash because of me.

I wanted a baseball glove for Christmas. The one he picked up was not the one I wanted. Like an ass, I complained. Dad got in the car. It was a white-out. He drove to the only place he knew where he could

77

get an Ozzie Smith glove: Cherry Ridge. He drove over the Dam, lost control on the ice and wrecked. He was trapped inside, too injured to move, and bled to death. It was my fault.

I'm so sorry, Dad. I'm fighting. I'm fighting so hard to keep this dead world alive. Mom misses you. Some days I have hope she'll get better. And then there are days like today, where that's blown out. I miss you, Dad. I miss you so much. I know you never allow me to think it, but there is a part of me that will forever feel you're not here because of me. I'm never going to give up on the world you once built here. Not because I have to, because I want to. I want to be a son you would be proud of again. It's just... I just... I don't have the answer all the time. If only... I wish... what would you do, Dad? I can't do this by myself anymore. Just give me something. One sign. One glimmer. One light.

A few days pass and it's Thursday night. A light shines from Rose's dad's window. Rose's dad, Jimmy Punch, begins to appear as my eyes adjust. He's huge, I'll give him that. There he is, sitting on his bed, motionless, without a care in the world. His tie is loose, but his collared shirt stretches over his muscles. I can barely see his face from curled, furrowing eye brows. From what I can see, his chin is chiseled enough to be seen through a five o'clock shadow. I can't believe that's the badass from the Ashton highlights that's been haunting us for years.

That's Jimmy Punch? "The" Jimmy Punch?

Rose enters his bedroom. I jump to the floor. She pulls a steaming bowl of water and places it on his night-stand. She fills her hand with shaving foam and lathers his neck, chin, and cheeks. In delicate strokes, she moves his head this way and that, as she drags a barber's blade across his face and up and down his neck. Once finished with the neck, she fills an empty table glass with whiskey and hands it to him while she finishes his face. She leaves and returns, scrubbing her hands with gel and styles his hair. She runs to a closet, grabs a skinny, casual tie, places it around her neck, ties it, then takes it off and places it under his collar. She takes a step back, sizes him up like a sculpture, and after an approving shake of the head she pulls a phone out of her pocket, dials, and within moments, headlights of a car pull into the driveway. I crouch, but can still see Rose.

She pours another glass, pushes it to his mouth, and once he finishes, she pulls him up by the armpits to get him to his feet. She takes his hand. Their porch light comes on and he walks out alone. The driver opens the back door for him. The car leaves.

Where does he go?

I watch the car all the way down the street until it turns towards town. I turn back and she's staring at me from the porch. But I don't move this time. She doesn't move. A staring "stand-still." She moves first by rolling her eyes and giving me a signal to open my window. I resist. She gives me a snarky face, turns around and heads into her dad's room. She reappears with a brick in her right hand. Juggling it up and down, she raises it to the side of her head in "ready to launch mode," totally calling my bluff. I open the window.

"Jesus, girl! What do you want?"

Placing the brick on the window sill, she says, "We need to talk."

"About what? Look, if it's about your Daddy issues, don't worry about it. I mean, it's a little weird how he's like your little toy doll, but I know what you're going through."

She blows a piece of hair off her forehead and grabs the bannister with both hands. "Because you, and the rest of the kids in this psycho-bin of a town, aren't the only ones with problems."

I'm taken aback a bit by her bluntness; she *does* make a good point. "Okay... easy, killer."

Relaxing her grip, she asks, "You want to come over for a bit?"

"Over there? Why? You gonna hit me with a bat this time? My jaw is still recovering, so I think I'll pass on the invite."

"Well, either you come over here, or I'm coming over there. Whichever way you choose, we're having a conversation about what the hell is going on in this town. Tonight."

I don't trust her. I can't just let her keep messing shit up. I head over.

Without a response, she turns, closes the door, and heads out of the room.

She leaves the porch light on. After climbing a few steps, I look for a doorbell. I see a knocker in the middle of a massive wooden door. But as I extend my hand, the sound of vault-like bars retract from its frame. Frozen, I stand as the door opens. Not a moment after I cross the threshold, the door slams shut, re-locking.

Inside, the house is a wooden palace. I can smell mahogany and fresh pine. This is one of the few nice homes left in Ashton. Ours isn't bad, but not as nice as this. To my left is a spiral staircase to the second floor. On my right, an untouched dining table set for dinner. A massive kitchen spreads the entire back corner, centered by an island stove that could sustain a restaurant. The middle of the room, however, draws my attention. A fire billows inside a glass case and lights the room. Within a few feet, I see that on top of the glass case is a stunning carved mantle acting as a stage for the four years of Powder Match trophies. Each has its own unique flare, but what remains constant is a glass-blown miniature of the entire valley. I'd heard rumors about the trophies being finely detailed. The urge to hold one is overpowering. I hear her voice from above. "Pretty cool, huh?"

Startled, I turn around and see Rose standing in the middle of the spiral staircase, leaning on the bannister. Two pigtails lie over her shoulders, resting over her chest. She's wearing a tank top and sweat pants. I say, "Uh… yeah. I've never seen one up close."

"Oh, no?" She walks down the stairs dragging one hand on the bannister. After finishing the final step, she turns and in a sarcastic tone says, "I thought that the almighty Jester knew everything about Ashton. Of course, he would know what a Powder Match trophy looks like."

Well, I haven't won one.

She says, "Relax. I'm just giving you a hard time. I knew you hadn't. There's a reason why this place is protected like an armored truck."

"So… so… these… these are the real trophies? Not replicas?"

"Yup, no joke. Want to hold one?"

"What? Really? You'd let me hold one?"

"Sure, why not? Dad doesn't remember much these days. He wouldn't notice if *I* was gone, let alone a trophy. Third from the left. The wooden one. It's my favorite."

I look down the mantle and on the far end stands the only one made of wood.

"Really? Why? The glass ones are so cool."

Standing on her tiptoes, she hands it to me and says, "It's the first one. The one that changed everything."

I can't believe it. The rumors are true. Every single aspect of the valley is carved in magnificent detail. I look down on my house like one of those satellite views from space. I can even see a still flag waving in front of our school. I attempt to touch the flag, but she stops me. "Careful, remember it's delicate."

I feel the power flow through each tip of my fingers. Then it hits me. I hand it back to her and ask, "Why are you showing this to me? You screwed things up. Irish fell for you and not Vivian. Well, he was kind of faking it with her, but that's not the point. I don't care if your dad is Jimmy Punch. I'm the one that has to go fight in the Snow Brawl."

She places the trophy back on the mantle and heads toward the island in the kitchen, expecting me to follow. She pulls out a barstool and walks to a small wooden cabinet where she takes out two shot glasses and a dusty bottle. After blowing dust off the top, she pours both glasses to the brim, and places one in front me. I look at the bottle and see the date: 1950.

She takes a shot like it's a sip of water and responds, "We have tons of bottles. Don't worry about it."

"Okay."

I take the shot and it's the best whiskey I've ever had.

She pulls out a pack of cig sticks from a drawer, packs the box in rotation, and tosses one in my direction. She lights one up for herself, and tosses the lighter to me.

"Thanks."

She crosses her legs and stares. "So you're the Jester? The famous wordsmith for the Irish. Or should I say *infamous?*"

I don't know what she means by that last part, but to keep things on an even keel, I respond, "Yes. That's my responsibility. My title. If that's what you mean."

She smirks and says, "And what does a Jester do?"

"I speak for Irish."

I drive my stool out and it screeches against the wood as I head towards the door. She demands, "Sit Down."

I stop and turn. With the tip of her slipper, she pushes the stool in my direction.

"Who do you think you are?" I ask. "First you're this nerdy girl that everyone feels sorry for because Vivian makes fun of you, then you're this hot-ass vixen that seduces both The Irish and everyone in the Hall. Now you're busting my chops. I'm no dope, girl."

She puts out her cig stick on the wooden counter and says, "I only know about this valley from my father's drunken rants, and things that I've heard in random conversations. I remember the fire Irish was talking about. Well, I remember the heat. But I always thought I was saved by a fireman or something. The polar bear triggered memories of my family. Mom and Clove live in Cherry Ridge and polar bear fleece is like gold to the Cherries.

"The bear triggered memories. Out of all the shit, I can't get the expression from Irish's face out of my head. He was fearless. His eyes were red and determined. He reminded me of a younger version of my dad. A younger version.

"I didn't mean to deceive anyone. I had to see it for myself. When I opened the doors at school on that first day, that intrigue turned into a dark reality. The stories I heard were tales of glory and wonder. Wonder is definitely the last word I would use to describe Ashton nowadays."

It's nice to get some answers. And her honesty is refreshing, but I still don't get the whole point of me being here.

"Say I believe you. Why do you need to talk to me? You have Irish in your hands. He's like butter when he talks about you. And while it does bother me a little, I'll be honest, you are… slightly… attractive… kind of… I guess… not my type… but I get it."

She giggles, grabs the bottle, and pours another. "Ha… thanks… I guess. I didn't mean to sound so demanding before, it just seems to be the only way to get one's attention around here."

I don't know what to say.

She begins again. "Look… I know I've messed things up a little bit—"

"A little bit!?"

You screwed up the entire plan!

"Well, a lot I guess. I'm sorry for that. But can you just give me few minutes? That's all. You can go after that."

"Fine."

Playing with the shot glass, she starts. "Jester, I know about the Powder Match. I know that the winner between Cherry Ridge and Ashton receives huge winnings. Twenty million is a lot of money. The Academia Trials, the Chute, the Snow Brawl... I get everything. But after all the stories, I look at those trophies and still don't get it."

"Don't get what?"

"Hey trust me, I would die for my dad, but he's not the intellectual type."

"I don't know what you're trying to say, or ask, Rose."

She pauses. Her eyes search for words.

"In order to win the games, a town must win two of the three events. We couldn't win the Chute because of the Cherries. That leaves Academia and the Snow Brawl. Obviously, the Snow Brawl was well taken care of by my dad, but the Academia part puzzles me."

"And?"

"A little over a year ago, my dad started to suffer these memory spells, and to help, I started searching through some old things, and I found something."

"What?"

She heads back to the mantle, grabs the wooden trophy, reaches under, and tears a picture from the base. She places the trophy on a foot table in front of the fire, heads towards me, sits back down, and holds the picture face down.

What is she hiding?

Her hand shakes. She tries to grab a cig stick from the box, but drops it. I pick it up off the table, place it in her mouth, and light it up. Taking a hit, she gathers herself.

"I want you to know we moved back here because I'm getting my brother and my mom back."

You want your family back? We all want our families back. What makes your situation any different?

I pour myself a straight drink from the bottle.

"You know, Rose. It isn't about you and your family. No one really has family anymore. Parental guidance is pretty limited in Ashton if you can't tell. Why is your family any different?"

Faced. Take that.

She pours herself a cold glass of water from the refrigerator dispenser.

She says, "After all the memories, stories, everything, there was always something missing. Even when Irish spoke at the meeting something was missing."

"Something? What do you mean?"

"Well, not something necessarily... someone."

She turns the picture over and it's from the day of the first winning of a Powder Match trophy. It's Jimmy, Mickey, and everyone cheering as if they just won an Olympic Gold.

I play dumb and ask, "Someone?"

She points to a kid, locked shoulder to shoulder with her father. A kid that looks just like me. She says, "This is his Jester. I didn't know about a Jester until we moved back home. I knew I recognized your face. It wasn't until that first day in the Hall that I figured it out. It wasn't just my dad that won all those trophies. He needed a Jester. And a damn good one at that."

"Screw all this cryptic shit, Rose, just say it, ask it, whatever."

"That's your dad isn't it?"

She thinks the picture is going to upset me, but I remain stone cold. I mudder under my breath, "So what? Big deal. So my dad was your dad's Jester."

With a soft voice, she says, "Well, I mean, what happened? If you don't mind me asking? I mean... I'm sorry... forget it."

Fury inside me builds from head to toe, but once it hits my head, my eyes cry.

"He's dead. He's dead and it's because of me. That's all you need to know. Happy now? Get what you wanted? Can I go... highness?"

She doesn't respond.

"Screw it. I'm out of here."

I walk towards the door, and the bars open automatically. Before I can turn to give a sarcastic thank you, I see her running towards me.

She tears at the collar of my sweater and drags me behind a wall next to the staircase.

She covers my mouth with one hand while raising her finger to her lips with the other. The cackling sounds of laughter from an inebriated woman screech through the door. I notice the wooden trophy still resting on the table. I run out of Rose's grasp to the middle of the room. She whispers in agitation, "Forget it! J! It doesn't matter! Get back here!"

"One second."

"J! You don't understand! Dad… he's like your…"

"Like my what?"

"Your mom. He's like your mom at dinner!"

"My mom? What do you know about my—"

"I watch too."

I hear a much deeper voice than Rose's.

"Jester? Is that you?" the voice asks.

Rose drops her chin to her chest. Turning to my left, I see a towering figure standing outside the doorway, blocking most of the light from the porch. It's Jimmy's face in shadow. His broad shoulders stretch to within inches of both ends of the door frame. I smell the crisp smoke from the fire. He takes a step forward. A pretty young woman, some girl he picked up at the bar, maybe in her early twenties, tries to get his attention. With her right hand, she grabs his bicep, but her hand looks like a newborn's grabbing a finger. Before she can even say anything, the door slams in her face as he enters the house.

Lit by the flickering fire, he walks towards me. It's as if with each step he expands. My body hardens by the second. He approaches. I tilt my head to meet his eyes. His breathing is heavy. The stench of oak-barreled whiskey billows down. Crouching to a knee, he almost falls over, but catches himself with his left arm. Within inches of my face, in a gurgled, torn voice, he says, "Ho-Ho-Holy shit! Jester? It is you!"

I turn from a statue into a raggedy doll as he grabs my shoulders and lifts me to his face. My legs dangle. I'm able to see his eyes and his eyes are terrifying, like two black olives floating in a Bloody Mary. Fighting my fear, I wait for him to move. Nothing. Terrified seconds pass. He puts me down and places a bear paw on my shoulder. He moves the paw to my neck. He pulls my head towards the kitchen, saying, "Man… Jester… where have you been? You should have told me you were coming over. I would have waited for you."

I turn around, looking back to Rose. She's gone. I don't know what to do. I don't know what to say. Then I remember Rose's words, "… like your Mom."

PTSD.

I try my best to act as if I'm coming home to a finished puzzle and respond, "Sorry, man. I guess it was just a surprise."

He points at me with a winking smile saying, "You and your surprises, man. That's what makes you the best. Those damn Cherries never knew what they had coming. Come on, let's have a drink."

"I'm kind of tired."

He looks down at me. "Tired? Who are you?"

My heart drops. But he catches it with a smile saying, "Oh… I get it… now that we're parents and all, we can't have a few drinks? To hell with that noise. We're having a drink for old times." Cupping his hand around the side of his mouth, he bellows, "Rosey! Get down here! We have a guest."

I try to stop him.

"You don't have to do that. I'll get it for us," I say.

"Nonsense. She loves staying up late hearing about old stories. Rosey!"

Her voice screams back, "All right! All right! I'm coming!"

She heads down the stairs and when she comes into view of the kitchen, she's changed her clothes. Swaddled in a huge sweatshirt, with pigtails draped on her shoulders, she looks younger.

"Hey, Dad," she says with her head down.

Ignoring her reluctance, he commands, "Sweetie, would you please get a fresh pack of cigarettes and the finest bottle of wine for my friend and me?"

She says, "Sure, Dad." But before she turns to the cabinet, she looks at me and asks him, "What's the special occasion?"

Grabbing his belly, he slams my back, laughing.

"I guess we're getting older. Sweetie? You don't recognize who this is? Remember you used to play with his son at the park? It's my Jester, Jay. This valley is ours. Well, not all of it."

He tears up.

"Damn Cherries took my son and my girl."

Clove... I almost forgot about him. Then there's the mom.

"What?" I ask.

"Your memory is shit too? Must have been all those brawls. Because Jameson is a Cherry, she had to choose between Clove or Rose and me. Clove was her choice."

He throws a fist to the counter, spraying dust in the air.

Rose walks over to me, opens her hand, and looks up at me with empty eyes and says, "I apologize, Jester, sir. It's so very nice to meet you."

When I look at her, I feel a weird connection. Like she's a part of the Ashton family. I respond, "Don't worry about it. Rose, is it?"

When the words come out, her response is confusion and surprise. Which is exactly how I feel as well.

"Um... um... yes, sir," Rose says.

Sir?

She heads to the closet from which she pulled *our* bottle, but he stops her and commands, "Not that garbage, Rose. The real stuff. From the homeland, in the cellar."

She looks back at him, then to me, mouthing me a silent apology, and she heads to the cellar, leaving me alone with him. He waits until she leaves the room and pulls out a flask to take a swig and hands it to me. I take a fake sip, attempting to stay as sober as possible. He takes a deep breath, and sways his head back and forth staring at the empty stairway to the cellar before saying, "Man... isn't she beautiful? Jesus. I don't know what I'm going to do when she gets older, ya know?"

I haven't the slightest clue what to say. I try to think of what Dad would say, but my mind turns blank. A line comes up and without a thought, I say, "I wouldn't worry about it. I'm sure you'll figure it out. Just make sure she doesn't date a guy like you."

I prepare for the worst, but he laughs and takes another sip.

"Ha! True, true, at least you got a son." Cracking his knuckles, he says, "I don't know how I'm not going to kill her first boyfriend."

It'd be a good fight.

"Ha. You and every other father on this planet."

He laughs again and my fear settles, and it feels as if I'm talking to one of my friends.

Rose comes back from the cellar with a much smaller bottle. Instead of dust, it's blanketed in spider webs. She wipes it off with a towel, grabs a bottle opener from a drawer, reaches away from her body, and twists the cork from the top of the bottle. It's wine. I've never had wine before. It's mom's drink.

I ask him, "Jimmy, how old is this?"

"I actually don't know. It was a gift given to me from Seamus. Supposed to be from the Civil War. I guess there was a troop of Irishmen led by a brilliant drunk, I forget his name, but they were called The Irish Brigade. I guess it was some heroic battle or something."

"And Seamus gave this to you?"

"Me? He gave it to us, remember? When you cleaned house in Academia, leaving the Cherries behind. We killed them in The Snow Brawl and broke the shackles. You and me, man, together. We did it. I guess Seamus felt we deserved it."

Raising our glasses to cheers, I look to Rose and her eyes are still cold. I raise my glass and before we cheer, he chants, "To the old and the new, the green and the blue, true Irish we two, me and you. Forever, brother." Clinking the glass against the wood, I follow, and together we drink.

It's sour, but after a few sips, goes down smooth. I guess they hadn't quite refined the process over a hundred years ago. After I gag, he bellows again, "Ha-ha… always a lightweight." He finds the pack of cig sticks on the table and places one in his mouth. He searches his pockets for a lighter. Before he reaches into his back pocket, Rose sprints to his side to light the cig stick.

After a hit, he speaks. "Geez, thanks, Sweetie. Hey! When are they going to have my lighter fixed? It feels like it's been years."

Irish has his lighter.

Rose looks to me shaking her head and says, "Just need to fill it up with some butane. Any day now, Dad."

He elbows me in the shoulder. "Better be. Jesus. You'd think years of money would get some respect around here, ya know?

"Ha, yeah, I guess," I say.

After a few puffs in silence, his jubilation turns real. The tone of his voice turns like a brother's as he asks, "No, but seriously man, can I be honest?"

I look to Rose. She gives a shrug in confusion.

I look to him. "Sure, what's up?"

Instead of filling the glass, he takes a swig and says, "You know, even after all the awards, parties, girls, and drugs, nothing's better than watching your son and my Clove playing baseball." A tear drops from the crease of his eye. "Rose sitting next to me, smearing her face with cotton candy, cheering on her twin brother." He places his hand on the side of my face. "Just think. Our kids could save this place."

Courage takes over and I ask, "What happened? I mean, what happened after the fire?"

I look to Rose. She covers her mouth with wide-watered-eyes. He looks to Rose and starts to cry.

"I had to, Jay. I had to leave. If the Berries caught us, they would have done anything to keep me in jail for my third strike. The Cherries weren't going to allow Rose and Clove to live together. After the fire, we headed to the eastern drought lands with all the water we could store. It's terrible out there, Jay. Without water, there's no hope. At least there's hope in Powder Valley. We have hope."

A lot can happen in six years, Jimmy. Hopeful is the last word I would use to describe Ashton now.

Rose notices his tears and looks for something to wipe his eyes. She runs over with a napkin. With slight embarrassment, he says, "Jesus man, that fire. It's like the sun." Placing the napkin on the table he says, "Oh yeah, by the way, did you get the game glove you want for Jeremiah? You know the one you were looking for. I hope it's the right one."

"Glove? Um… yeah… I'm sorry, glove?"

Pain, confusion, relief, and elation surge through me. I can't believe that glove, *my* glove, is an Ozzie glove. A game glove. One of the best to ever play. It's in my room. It's in my room because of Dad… because of Dad.

I'm about to lose it.

We're going to have a crying fest.

He attempts to stand up, slips off his stool, and careens backwards to the floor and slams the back of his head. We rush to help him, scared. His eyes closed, I slap him once, and he opens his eyes in confusion and embarrassment.

Eventually, we're able to drag him to the couch in front of the fire. Feels like he weighs as much as a dead bull. Before Rose returns with a blanket, he's in and out of snoring. She tucks him in, leaves a glass of cold water and a beer on the table next to him. Thoughts of Dad, Mom, Irish, Rose, and Ashton storm my mind. I attempt to grasp what just happened. I ask her, "Can I go now?" and head to the door. She stops me.

"I'm sorry, Jester."

"Sorry about what?"

She turns me around and holds both of my hands.

She says, "Everything. Your life sucks and I've just made things worse."

Her eyes water.

"I'm sorry about Clove and your mom, Rose," I say.

She wipes away a tear.

"He's not gone. And neither is my Mom. We don't have much more time."

She pulls me close.

"What?" I ask.

She pushes me away to give a moment to breathe, and says, "Why not now? What if we win now?"

"What? Now? That's not happening."

"How come? Why can't it happen?"

Her confidence is overwhelming. At first, I thought she was asking me *if* we could win. But her eyes don't look weak. She's not asking me.

"I mean, win the games and take the money. Take this valley over for ourselves," she says.

"Rose… we lose every year in Academia. I don't know if you've noticed, Ashton doesn't really have the best "school" supplies. I try in Academia, but it's usually five to one and I can't take down all of the Cherries. Plus, why would the kids of the Academic Hall want to help us after all that Gauntlet bullshit? Vivian is our only chance in the

90

Chute. Your and Irish's love affair has already put that in jeopardy. We have to fight again."

"Damn man... *you're* our Jester? No wonder this place sucks. Would it help if I get some kids in Academia? The Academic kids don't want to go outside the valley into the desert just like everyone else."

"Maybe," I respond.

"I'll see what I can do," she says.

"I don't think you quite understand. This isn't a, 'see what I can do' situation, Rose."

"I'm serious. You want to know something about all the stories I've heard from Dad? They never talk about celebration... the party... the money. I wasn't lying when I said my dad didn't care about the trophies. Every story I've heard, it's about one thing."

"What's that?" I ask.

She grabs my shoulders and says, "The fight. Look how happy they were. It didn't matter if they won. You saw my dad. I've never seen him like that."

"Rose, trust me, the Snow Brawl isn't fun. The Cherries beat the shit out of us. We just don't have the ability to win."

"What if we can improve the odds?" she asks.

"What do you mean?"

"What about Christmas Daye?"

Christi? What about her?

Rose releases my shoulders. She walks over and stares in the fire and continues.

"Some of the kids in the cafeteria were huddled around a table watching her videos. She's a really good snowboarder, right?"

"Well, kind of. She only does stuff in town, like tricks and stuff. We're not allowed on the mountain."

She turns around and says, "But she could still get down the mountain?"

"I'm not throwing Christi down the Chute for nothing."

She's thrown aback and says, "*Nothing*? Winning the Powder Match is not *nothing*."

"And winning the Powder Match isn't your only agenda. Spit it out."

She can't hold back her tears before saying, "I want my family back. You heard my dad. Clove and Mom are just over the Dam and we can't even see them. It's twisted."

It is a tragedy. But life is tragedy. I have learned that much. I need a drink.

"What if I can get you a practice slope on a mountain?" she asks.

Now, I'm curious…

"And how do you plan on going about that?"

She moves close to me and speaks with a precise and conservative tone. "My old house. Mom and Clove's house in Cherry Ridge. The backyard has a mountain slope."

She's crazy.

"Like the Berries are just going to turn a blind eye to your Dad being in town when they hear about us messing around with Clove and your Mom."

She bites her fingernails, thinking.

"I didn't say I had a perfect plan. That's why I need your help," she says.

I look her in the eyes.

"You're playing with a lot of lives here. We have more to think about than just our own."

"What 'lives'?"

She's right. What life is this?

"Then let's change it," we say at the same time.

"I get a mountain and you get Christmas. But you're right, J. I know I can find a slope for Christmas. I need your help to get her there," she says.

Shea.

"Shea. My friend, Shea, can help us."

"He can sneak us in?"

"Look, I said he could 'help' us get there."

"Great!"

I say, "It's Christi, though. She's not that type."

"Wait a minute, she's not *what* type?"

"All I'm saying is the Chute isn't just a few jumps down a little hill. It's serious shit. The only person Christi's done tricks in front of is her little brother."

"So what if the only person who's seen her is her little brother? What does that matter?"

"It matters… it matters because I don't want to see her get hurt."

"You don't want to see her get hurt?"

"I meant we. Irish and me."

She shakes her head and contests, "No, you didn't. You said, 'I' don't want to see her get hurt.' And you didn't call her Christmas, you said 'Christi.'" She places both hands behind her back as if she's stepped away from checkmate and continues, "That's not the only thing I've heard about Christmas Daye."

"What else have you heard?"

"Well, it's not that I've heard anything directly."

"Stop playing."

"Fine… despite your complete ignorance of the existence of the Academic Hall, quite a few girls have said Jester is the real Bachelor of Ashton, not Irish."

"Shut up."

"No joke." She drags a finger down her cheek resembling a tear and frowns saying, "And they're just so darn jealous of this Christmas girl who has stolen his heart."

"So what? This whole town is a cesspool for drama. Get to your point."

"Christmas deserves a chance just like anyone and you're worried about her feelings being hurt."

"That's not what I meant—"

"It may not be what you meant, but it's how it is." She pulls the trophy picture from her front pocket and displays it in front of me. "We need Christmas."

"And how are we supposed to do that?"

She raises her fist to me ready to strike, thinking it was a joke.

I wince. "No… No… No… I'm serious, Rose."

She pushes me to the door.

"You're going to ask her out."

I laugh.

"Yeah right."

The door-bars retract.

"Nope… nope… nope… can't let you do that. We need something drastic. Something now. We need her. You're the only person around. You need to do it."

"Nope. Never asked a girl out before. Too bad."

"Better figure it out. Grow a pair."

The door opens without her saying anything. It shuts behind me. I walk to my house and see the living room light through our window. I shoot through the door to find Mom. My entrance startles her. She says, "Jesus, J.! You scared me."

"Mom? Is that you?"

She sits with a blanket over her shoulders, turns back to the foot table in front of her, and asks, "What? Of course it is, silly. Who else would it be?"

Looking over her shoulder, I see a half-empty wine glass as she holds a puzzle piece in her hand. My heart skips a beat, and I ask, "Tough puzzle, huh Mom?"

"Yeah, it is! I just can't seem to get past the smoke over our factory."

I look at the picture on the puzzle box. Rose's photo flashes in my mind.

I look down at Mom, sit down, hug her and give her a kiss on the cheek.

"I love you, Mom."

"I love you too, J."

I reach over to the lamp next to me. "Here, Mom. Let's turn on some more light."

PART II.

FRESH POWDER

14.

PANIC ATTACK

POWDER MATCH: 43 DAYS

I SWEAT BULLETS FOR DAYS stressing about asking Christi out. Christi is not just any girl, she's basically perfect. And I couldn't be further from perfect. I have always been curious about what she would be like to date. I can't help looking at my massive scar everywhere I go. Her rejection would suck.

What would Irish do? Be big, strong, handsome, and not a wuss.

It takes me a week to man up and ask Christi out.

A crisp breeze crawls through my ears while my body trembles in a cold sweat like being showered in melted ice. My eyes awake to dissipating wisps of breath. Clenching the fabric to my neck, I fight to sustain the incubated warmth that kept me alive through the night. The breeze crawls again from my left side and with a painful, delicate turn, I see my window left open from the night before. Memories burst through my head, creating a nauseous surge to my stomach. After a wave of dry heaves, I force myself to the window. Grasping the frozen frame, my fingers ache like brittle icicles fighting to stay firm. I pull downward. As the airway is sealed, the glass turns to fog and crystalizes. I rub the window in an attempt to keep a small visual to Rose's house, but the ice is opaque. Our furnace growls as it ignites. I stand next to the floor vent and warmth comes to my feet and my body.

Visions from last week ache like my very first hangover. Rose, Jimmy, Dad, Mom, and everything else pound like picks into stone. Holding on to the railing, I contemplate lying in the fetal position and faking sick until I hear Mom screech, "Hey! Sandman! You're lucky we got hit with a freeze over last night and got a late start. It's already 8:30 and the news says school starts at 9:30. Irish will be here in a minute. I'm taking the truck. Have a good day!" Mom is back to her sober self.

Before I can say anything, the garage door opens and shuts, blowing a cool breeze throughout the house. I don't know if it's the breeze, or Mom, or whatever, but when the door closes, my mind turns to Christi.

I have to ask her out today.

A panic trigger hits. I run to the toilet and make myself retch to feel better. I need to vomit first. At least with alcohol, I get the reward of something coming out, but I don't even get a glimpse of stomach acid. After fighting to control a few breaths, I grab the corner of the sink to lift myself up to look in the mirror. My eyes are bloodshot and the bags underneath are heavy and purple. I open the drawer and with one hand holding my toothbrush and the other my toothpaste, I try to put them together, but the liquor-shakes turn them into opposing magnets. I slam both against the sink, look to my right at a cupboard, and think: last resort.

I open it up. Standing on the top of the shelf is a flask.

I have to.

I grab the flask, take a large gulp, and it's like swallowing fire. I cough to tears, but my stomach settles. After a few deep breaths and another sip, I turn on the faucet for my weekly shower, flask in hand. With my back to the wall and my head down, the trickles of water feels like a beaded massage, comforting me to reality. I drink again. I say to myself, "You can do this, J. We can do this, man. She's just a girl."

Christi is not just a girl.

"I know, all right? But we still have to do it." I lean back, take a huge breath, and let the massage run to my chest. My eyes get heavy. I pass out.

The water is freezing, but Irish screaming is what make me conscious. He bursts through the door.

"J.!" he hollers, pulling me out of the shower while covering me with a towel. He digs into my shoulders and throws my back to the wall again and again.

"J., man! Wake up! C'mon buddy."

I try to move. I can hear him, but can't respond.

He cocks a fist. "Sorry about this, man."

A wrecking ball blasts my jaw. Adrenaline courses through me. I throw him against the toilet.

My jaw aches like having a tooth pulled.

"What the hell?"

"Sorry, man… I didn't know what to do. I thought you were like dying or something."

"Why the hell would you think that?"

"Well, I thought something was off when you didn't come outside, so I texted, and called, and when you didn't answer, I thought something was up. So I came inside, yelled around, and still no response, until I heard the water running. I yelled again and nothing. I opened the bathroom door a little and saw your hand outside the curtains with an empty flask and now we're here."

"Really?"

He hands me a bottle of water. "Yeah, dude. What the hell is up?"

"Nothing."

He raises his fist again. "I'll hit you again if you don't tell me."

"Fine! I'll tell you. Can I get dressed first?"

"I'll be downstairs."

He closes the door.

I walk to the sink buzzed, but the anxiety has settled. I turn on the faucet and splash my face with a few hits of cold water. I look to the mirror, look at myself, and say, "You can do this, J. You can do this. It's time."

After brushing my teeth, I head to my room and look in my closet. *What would impress Christi?*

I don't really have too much to worry about because my hoodie covers up most of my shirt, but still, what color should I wear underneath? My favorite color is light blue. The color of her eyes, so I go with an old Denver Nuggets shirt.

I head downstairs. Irish is in the kitchen.

I zip up my hoodie.

"Sorry about that, man. I just had a really bad panic attack again this morning."

He puts a hand on my shoulder.

"Damn, man, seriously. I'll see what I can do the next time we make a run over to the factory, but why are you so stressed? We got a late start from the massive temperature drop last night. This should be a day to celebrate."

I have bigger problems, Irish.

This could be a good time to tell him about last weeks' show, but it's too heavy to handle right now. Plus, I can't get Christi out of my mind.

"It's Christmas," I say.

"Christmas? What about her?"

"Well, I like her. A lot."

"Yeah, dude. We all know."

"We? Who's we? Never mind that. I'm going to do it, Irish. I'm going to ask her out today."

With a shocked, elated smile, he asks, "No way! Seriously?"

"Yeah, I guess I thought about the way you were talking about Rose, and wanted to know what it would be like. Then this morning, all of a sudden, my stomach turned into a hot mess. Way different than before."

He smiles and a piece of tape rips from his laceration.

"Yeah, I know what you're saying, man. I get it too. It's like a terrible combination of being sick, nervous, and hungover. It sucks."

"I know, right?"

"But if there's one thing I can promise, not that the feeling goes away, but when she's there in front of you, it changes into something awesome. Like the best Sweets ever, mixed with adrenaline. It's wicked. You'll love it."

"Umm, yeah, that does sound cool, dude, but in case you didn't notice, Rose fell into your lap like some twisted long-lost love story. I actually have to ask Christmas out."

"Oh, shit. You're right. That does suck."

"You're a big help."

"Don't worry, man. You're the Jester. There isn't a girl in this school that would pass up a chance with you.

"I wouldn't worry about it. She's a good girl, you know. She's gorgeous, for sure, but not in a fake way like Vivian's Barbie doll bunch. Plus, she's like the nicest girl on the planet. That's why I liked sending her to Mars's bench. Get her away from Vivian before she could suck the life out of her."

"Great. So at the worst, I'll get a pity date."

"You know what I'm saying. If there was one guy I would want to date Christmas, it would be you, understand?"

I'm starting to like this new Irish. I actually feel better now.

"Thanks."

"No worries. Have you thought about when you're going to do it?"

"A little bit, but not really. I need some time to think it over."

"Sure, man, no worries."

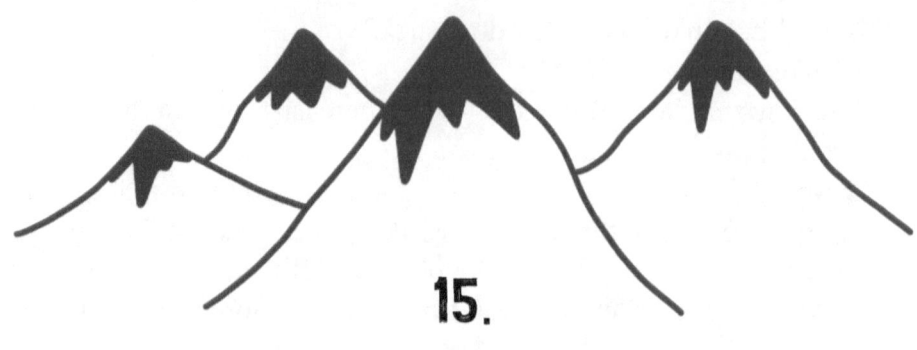

15.

WHAT BELLS?

I GRAB THE HEAVIEST WINTER coat I can find. We head outside and even though the air bites my face, I feel warm.

Irish's limo speeds through town, and in no time, he and I are sitting in the parking lot staring at the front of the school. The silence is comfortable, though, as if we're both prepping for a big game or something. He takes a deep breath, takes a pull out of his water bottle, and hands it to me. I push it away, but he grabs my wrist with his other hand. His face isn't angry; he's serious.

He says, "Trust me. She doesn't want to smell that shit on you."

He has me chug some mouthwash and watches me spit it out.

We run to the doors and once we're inside, the energy of the Hall takes over. Bench by bench, we make our rounds. I don't know if he does this on purpose, but Irish cuts the conversations short. We barely spend a minute at Mars's bench. I try not to look at Christi, but it's impossible. I turn my eyes and she's looking at me. She brushes away a wisp of blond hair. She sends a sweet smile. I smile back. The moment is perfect, but short-lived. Irish moves to the top Q.

We sit back down and normality hits. I look to Christi as she smiles and laughs on Mars's bench. She's stunning. I bet ice just melts away at her every step. I look to the clock. Just a few minutes to the bell. My hands are wet leather, not to mention the storms in my pits. In the last minute, I watch each second tick down.

Kids clear in waves towards the Academic Hall. Like in an old-time video game, I twist and turn around bodies, trying not to get hit, or lose her from my sight. She turns the corner as I escape from the swamp of people. I can't help myself staring at her angelic hair dancing down the small of her back to a Michaelangelo-esque molded ass.

Dammit, man, keep it together.

Deep breath after deep breath, time dissipates. The minute-warning bell is bound to ring. It's now or never. I reach to her shoulder with a gentle tap. Christi stops and turns around.

Her face lightens with some confusion. Her sweet, soft, high-pitched voice speaks to me. "Jester?"

What's wrong with you? You're the Jester. Man up.

"Hey Christi! Ummm… what's up?"

She giggles and the single dimple that I love appears on her right cheek when she says, "Ha… nothing. What's up with you?"

"Umm…"

Dammit man c'mon.

"Umm… I just wanted to say you look very nice today."

She blushes and brushes her hair. "Well, thank you, Jester. That's a nice surprise. So do you. I like your shirt. Blue is my favorite color."

Holy shit it worked.

I say, "Really? Me too. I—"

The warning bell rings.

"Well, I guess I better get going to class. It was nice talking to you." She turns away.

"Right… No, Christi wait!"

Turning back, she asks, "Yeah, Jester?"

"Christi… umm… I was wondering if… umm… if… you would like to come with me to the Hill sometime or whatever?"

She beams and points back to herself. "Me? You want me to go to the Hill with you?"

I look down at my feet and play with a stray shoelace.

"Well, yeah. I mean, it's no big deal if you don't want to, but if you did want to, it'd be nice."

"Of course! I would love to go with you!"

"You would?"

She punches me in the arm.

Ouch!

"Yes! I've been waiting. What took you so long?"

"Geez, just busy with things, I guess."

The final bell rings.

"Shoot. I'm tardy. My parents are going to kill me," she says.

"No worries. Here."

I pull one of Irish's passes out of my pocket and give it to her.

"Where did you get one of these?"

"Just one of the perks of being the Jester."

She jumps to me with a hug, and I melt from the smell of her strawberry shampoo.

"Thanks! Well, I guess I'll talk to you later or something."

"I was thinking I could get your number and text you later. It'd be nice to talk to someone other than Irish."

"Ha! Sure. Here."

She takes a purple glossy pen clipped between her cleavage. Trying not to get caught staring, I glance at the ceiling until she grabs my hand and writes her number.

"I guess I'll talk to you later then," I say.

"For sure, that'd be great. Have a good day, Jester."

"It's J. You can call me J. if you want."

"Okay J. See ya later."

As she walks away, I look to my hand and just as Irish said, the sickness in the pit of my stomach turns into the best thing I've ever felt. It's exactly like a painkiller adrenaline rush; maybe even better. I stand alone in the desolate hallway and it hits me. I'd given her my late pass. It's worth it.

The morning is a euphoric blur. After the lunch bell rings, I head to the limo, and Irish is already standing there with Curly and Mars, the three of them waiting like kids at an amusement park. Without letting me reach the limo, Irish walks to me and asks, "So did you do it?"

"Do what?"

"Shut up, dude. You know what I'm asking. Did you ask Christmas out?"

"Oh yeah… that I did."

"C'mon, dude. Spit it out. What did she say?"

"She said… she said, 'Yes,' man!"

He grabs both Curly and Mars by the shoulders. They look unhappy and sketch. "That's awesome, dude, I knew it. Right, fellas? I told you! Good for you, man. Well tell me all about it on the way to the Bridge. Drinks on me."

"Irish, they're always on you."

"I know, but I still like to say it."

The ride over is something different. It's like we're on a new level. A brighter level. When I tell him about the feeling after getting her number, he jumps in and tells me about his walk with Rose and spending time with kids outside of the Hall at lunch. We talk about something besides business and it's pretty cool. It's like there's a different side to us now. Something more than just surviving. Maybe Rose is on to something.

We reach the Bridge and once we enter, the new energy vanishes. We put our masks back on.

We enter and head to our respective booths. It's like Christi's moving to Five-Points. I hate it. But even still, as we shoot the shit and knock back a few, Christi and I take turns looking at each other like we're hiding our own little secret. I send her the first text.

Me: What's up?

Christi: Nothing, you?

Me: Nothing… just saying it's kind of awkward when you stare at me all the time. It's a bit clingy… LOL.

Christi: Shut up… you know you like it. BTW. There's a little bit of drool dripping from your chin.

I look across the pub and see her laughing.

Me: All right… you got me. Well, just wanted to say hi. Let me know if they give you any trouble over there. Mars is my boy. But you never know with people from Five-Points. They can get a little crazy.

Christi: Oh they're fine… they're actually really funny and everyone's been nice, for the most part. First days were weird, but it's kind of cool to hang out with people from across town. Thanks though. TTYL.

Me: **Later.**

The rest of the day is normal. The hardest part was not texting Christi. I can't get her off my mind. I wish this feeling would stay forever. I make it to the end of the day. It wasn't until the ride home with the Brigade that I remembered I hadn't told Irish about the date, when he asks, "So what are you going to do?"

Mars interjects. "Yeah J. What are you going to do?"

"What do you mean?"

Mars says, "Like, for the date. I mean, it's not like Ashton is a hot spot for love."

Irish whacks Mars. This part is going to be tricky.

"Well, that was the part I didn't quite tell all of you."

"What do you mean?" Irish asks.

"Don't get mad, promise?"

"Well, we're not making that promise," Irish says. "But I will get mad if you don't tell me."

"I invited her to the Hill."

The limo stops. With the front window down even Benny and Shea are listening in.

"What!? Why did you do that? That's between us mates. The Hill is for the Brigade! What were you thinking?" Irish asks.

All eyes in the limo are judging me.

I'm surrounded.

"Well, maybe if you brought Rose along too it would be cool, you know?"

Mars jumps in, "Now we gots two tricks messin' shit up. Are we just giving up on the plan? Screw the Powder Match. Let you two fall in love? With Vivian's blessing? Should I tell the families in Five-Points to start packing?"

Curly follows: "It's true J., I don't usually care about this shit. But that third strike keeps me up at night. It'd be dope to not have to deal those Sweets to the Cherries."

Irish says, "Okay J. Curly doesn't want to mess with the Cherries. I'm already playing with fire even talking to Rose. We can't mess up that agreement with Vivian and her family, remember. We're out of money. I can't just show up in public with Rose."

"Maybe there's a way you can," I say.

"What do you mean?" Irish asks.

Mars and Curly say at the same time, "Yeah J., tell us your master plan."

"Look, before I mention the next part, remember, I'm the Jester. This is my job. To think shit up."

Irish lights up a cig stick and grimaces. "Okay."

I say, "So, Irish, last night Rose and I were talking."

"You were talking? About what? What the hell, man?"

"She's my next-door neighbor. She threatened to break my window with a brick if I didn't talk to her. She's a hard-ass, dude. She doesn't ask permission to jump into your shit."

The smile from earlier returns to his face. "Really?"

"Yeah dude, remember, she's the daughter of Jimmy Punch."

The limo turns more silent if at all possible. Curly and Mars ask together, "She is?"

Through the side of his mouth, Irish says, "Well, that was supposed to be between J. and me. I guess I always knew, but just didn't want to think about it. Have you met him?"

I lie. "Hell no. You think I'm just going to bring my mother's cookies over and invite him in? That dude is terrifying. But Rose takes care of him. Does stuff for him. So, if she has something to say, I'm going to listen."

"So what did she say? And how does it involve me?" Irish asks.

"Well, to be honest, I don't know the whole plan, so I think you should talk to her first, but I can give you the gist."

"Okay."

I ask, "What if Vivian isn't the Queen of the Hall anymore?"

"What? You may have had a little too much to drink today, man. That's crazy talk."

"I'm serious, dude."

The gazes in the limo dart back-and-forth across as Irish contemplates in silence.

He waits. It takes minutes. Finally, Irish asks.

"Okay, say we do demote Vivian… who do we replace her with? Rose?"

107

"Nah, she not's really a snowboarder. That's probably not the best idea."

"Then who?"

"We replace her with Christmas."

"Christmas? What the hell, man? You just asked her out. Why the hell would we do that?"

"Christmas can do it, and once she's in, we'll still run the show, and then you'll be free to date Rose."

He shakes his head. "Now I'm listening."

Mars asks, "And what about Vivian? Her family still runs the plant. We have to keep her happy, remember?"

"That's the risk. We lose her. But if we win the Powder Match, then we won't need Vivian or her family. We'll be set for years. Give the Cherries a run for their money."

Curly asks, "Again, bruh, all good to hear, but how?"

I say, "Christmas wins the Chute."

Benny and Shea turn around, while Curly and Mars interject. "Shit. We're screwed," they say under their breath.

Irish asks, "And how are you going to get Christmas Daye to win the Chute? She hasn't even been on a mountain. That's a lot to put on her."

"I know. I haven't seen any video, but the Nerds talk about her all the time. If there's any downtime between classes, the Nerds immerse themselves in their phones. It's like she's their hope. There's something about a girl who's willing to break herself jumping off buildings on a snowboard. I don't have the balls to do that. Do you?" I ask.

Irish laughs. "Ha, okay, that's true. I'll talk to Rose tonight and get the rest of the plan. Let me sleep on it."

The fellas turn around and pull their hoods up in silence.

"Thanks." I finish.

We pull up into my driveway and as I get out of the car Irish says, "J. ..."

"Yeah, man."

"Enjoy your night. Congrats with Christmas. If this works out, you'll be dating The Queen."

"Shut up, man. See you tomorrow."

16.

ALL IN

POWDER MATCH: 42 DAYS

I GET A TEXT THE next day.

Irish: **Wake up ass... I'm in.**

The temperatures have risen and the ice is gone when I walk to Irish's limo. I get in to see Rose sitting with Irish. She looks at me with a sly smile and waves.

I see their hands together.

"Ahhh, isn't this cute," I say. "What's going on?"

"Easy, killer," she says. "I'm not taking your precious little seat. My ride is on its way. Figured it be best to just clear the air and get things straight."

"Okay. So you know the plan?" I ask.

"Yeah, I think it could work. But don't think I'm not pissed that you didn't me tell the whole plan yesterday," Irish interjects.

"It's not my plan to tell."

His face reddens. The angry Irish is back. "No more secrets. Between any of us. You hear me?!" he threatens.

Caressing her thumb across his palm, Rose interrupts. "Well, we don't have to tell each other everything we do. Do we?"

"Well not everything, but involving the plan and shit."

"Deal."

"Deal."

Rose speaks again. "So now that we're all in, let's see where we're at. First, Jester, nice job with Christmas."

"Yeah, it sucked big time asking her out. I hope I never have to do it again."

Irish says, "Yeah, he almost drank himself to death to get the courage."

"Shut up."

I punch him, which I immediately regret because it's like jamming my fist into a wall.

"Anyways, Rose, I want to say thanks for pushing me to do that. She's been really cool to talk to. She's actually pretty funny, too."

"Great! So next step, Jester?"

"Well, I was thinking about that. In order to get the Hall to stand firm for the replacement we need the heads of each Quarter. Curly just wants to win and Mars would probably like his sister back with the Five-Points Quarter. Benny and the underclassmen will cave with those two. There's only one person we're going to need and that may be an issue."

"Who?" Rose asks.

Before I'm able to say, Irish interjects. "Shea, he's talking about Shea."

"Shea?" she asks.

"Yeah. He's a true blood. Generational. His family has been in Ashton since the old days. So, he knows this valley in and out. He would die before seeing the Cherries take it over. He's a good guy, but a loose cannon. It won't be easy convincing him to take such a big risk by replacing Vivian with Christmas in the Chute."

"I'll take care of it," Irish says.

"Okay. Great! That's settled. I'll work with the academic kids. Jester, are you ready?" Rose asks.

"Ready for what?"

"Christmas."

"Oh yeah. We're just talking right now, so it may take a little bit to drop the idea. But I think she'll be into it. She hates Vivian."

"Good. The Chute is in a little over a month. We don't have much time. We all good?"

He looks to me. We nod.

A black car pulls up next to us. "Sweet!" Rose says while giving Irish a peck on the cheek.

She jumps out of the limo, into the black car, and heads off.

I raise my fist in a salute of solidarity. "You ready, man?"

He salutes back. "Let's do this."

17.

DRUNK UNCLE

POWDER MATCH: 39 DAYS

I**T'S FRIDAY NIGHT**. Irish loans us the limo for the Hill. Benny turns the engine off and walks away with a few cig sticks. Christi sits next to me smelling of cotton candy. She's braided her blonde hair in pigtails and tucked them under a white beanie. With a light blue sweater and white collared shirt underneath, her combination of tops and jeans makes me sweat with desire. She's awesome. I pour myself a drink.

"Want one?" I ask.

Christi scowls. "Take me home."

"What?" I respond.

"You heard me. You smell like my drunk uncle."

She moves to the seat across from me.

"We're kind of stuck here until Benny comes back," I say.

Focus, J. There's more to this than just Christi.

I pour my drink out the window, and open the limo fridge. Inside is a bottle of sparkling water and the polar bear I had given Rose with a small card from Irish saying, "Good luck, bro."

He can always get things.

I pour two glasses of water and give her one.

She says, "Sparkling water? My family barely has enough water for cold showers. How did you get this?"

"Irish left it for us."

She takes sip. "Oh. How do you drink it?"

"Just like normal water, I've had it a few times. Irish saves it for special occasions."

She gulps the glass, but chokes on the carbonation. I can't help myself from giggling. It's cute.

"Shut up," she says, "I didn't mean to judge you about your drinking?"

"It sounds like you were judging *me*," I interrupt.

"All I'm saying is… it would be nice if you weren't hammered on our first date."

I'm not hammered.

"Okay," I say.

We sit in painful silence. She holds her purse in her lap, tapping her fingers along its side.

Say something. Shit. Shit. Shit. Shit.

I look at her. We share a nervous smile together. She clears her throat. Again she coughs. Sweat beads on her nose.

"Nervous?" I ask.

"Kind of," she says with a shrug.

"Me too. I do the same thing when I'm nervous."

Her fingers tap across her purse. When she notices that I notice, her fingers hold still.

"You were tapping your fingers on your purse."

She drops her purse on the seat. "No, I wasn't."

"Yes you were. Trust me. Coming from someone who deals with anxiety every day, you were tapping your fingers."

I reach in the fridge and hand her the polar bear. "Here." I say, "Brush it's fur. It helps for some reason."

"You really get nervous?" she asks.

How much time you got? I'm dying right now.

I can't help myself from laughing. "Ha, that's an understatement."

Christi sips from her glass and says, "You don't have to be nervous around me."

"Easy for you to say. You don't have to be nervous around *me*."

She moves soft and gentle next to me, raises her hand, and with a cute innocence says, "My name is Christmas Daye. It's nice to meet you."

She's adorable. Mars was right about her brightening the air. That's right... Five-Points.

"It's nice to meet you, I'm Jes—, Jeremiah Connelly. How's the Five-Points Quarter treating you, Christi?"

She grabs my leg in excitement and spurts out sentences.

"I love Five-Points! I mean... it's not the nicest of areas, but when it snows, there's going to be like fifty new places to do snowboard tricks."

She's such a badass.

"I don't know how you do it. Some of those tricks are sick, for sure."

She responds with a humble, "Thanks. Can I ask you something?"

"Sure."

"Did that hurt?"

She points to her own face to indicate my scar.

Dammit. Of course she would say something, you ugly fool.

"It hurt more after," I say. "I had to eat through a tube for weeks from the broken jaw."

"That guy, Sonny, really did a number on you."

"Twitch got it worse. I'd rather not talk about it."

She looks down and brushes the back of the bear asking, "Okay. I don't know how you do it."

"Do what?"

"Compete in front of the whole world. I couldn't answer like one of those questions, and I consider myself to be pretty smart. Then the whole Snow Brawl thing. Puke."

She points to her mouth like she's about to vomit.

"It's probably the same with you and your tricks. I don't really think about it that much."

She moves in closer. "What do you think about then?"

Is this happening. Holy shit. Be smooth. Be smooth.

I grab her hand and say, "Us."

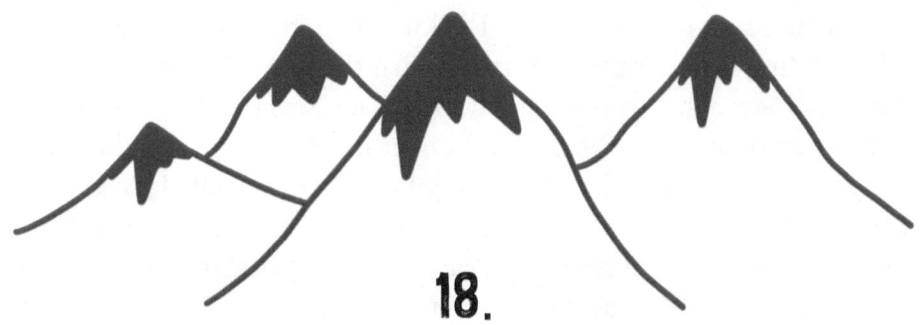

18.

CHRISTMAS SNOW

POWDER MATCH: 20 DAYS

I'VE HEARD LOVE STORIES, but living a love dream is entirely different. I think about Christi all the time. I've been writing her name on my notebook and I'm already in the hundreds. We've only been dating a couple of weeks or so. The first few dates were terrifying and a little awkward, but Christi always finds a way to clear the air with some jab or a sarcastic insult. It's hard to concentrate. When I'm with her it's like we're in a snow globe filled with magical glittering snowflakes. And when I'm not around her, all I can think about is the next thing I'm going to do to make her smile. But today is the day that I shake the globe.

A rare afternoon sun melts over the west peaks, turning the blue sky to orange and pink sherbet. Christi's family lives in my neighborhood. I walk up to her house and ice crackles under my shoes at each step. Approaching the porch, I see through a well-lit window a huge man leaning back in a recliner, with July, Christi's five-year-old sister, playing with toys on the carpet. Her mom walks in with mugs of beer, hands him one, and sits on the couch with a crossword puzzle. I'm envious. But after getting to know Christi, I can't think of anyone who deserves a normal family more than her. I wait a few more minutes to let them enjoy a few sips and relax. I take a deep breath and reach for the doorbell.

Footsteps patter to the door. The knob twitches and I'm certain it's July standing on her tiptoes trying to turn the knob. It turns and once it opens, I see Mr. Daye. A massive man, he towers a foot above me. Taller than Irish, and his belly swells over his waist; however, he's anything but menacing. He's all St. Nick jolly. His face is unbalanced from a broken nose he must have suffered during his football days. With wide eyes and a gleeful smile, he boasts, "Jester! Good to see ya, mate!"

I reach for a shake of the hand, but he pulls me in and presses my face to the top of his belly. He grabs the back of my head and ushers me into the room and says, "What'll we be drinking, my good boy! Anything on the house!"

Rum, please.

"Just a water, sir."

He turns to his wife and says, "My lady, would you please gather a fresh water for our dear Jester."

"It would be my honor, sir Jester," she responds.

"Mrs. Daye, please, you don't have to say 'sir.' Jester is fine."

"Oh, stop it, Sweetie! Anything for our Jester! Coming right up!"

Mr. Daye hauls me by the neck, into the living room. He forces me onto the couch and sits beside me to watch the football game.

"Can you believe the damn Broncos this year? Always screwing up. Ain't like the old days. Bunch of losers, you know."

A 3D flat screen television is mounted on a wall. I look to the score; the Denver Broncos are losing. I sit back, look to my right, and he stares at me for a comment. I haven't been able to follow the season. It's usually the highlight of our week, but Christi is my new highlight, so I just affirm his statement. "Yeah, I know. At least you were alive during their last Super Bowl win. All we get are highlights from the library, and it doesn't even have sound."

Mrs. Daye brings me a glass. Before I can take a sip, she raises her own saying, "To him who speaks and protects the weak. To him who saves and carries our graves. Our Jester he be. We are blessed for thee."

I've never gotten used to hearing the toast. I don't really care much when it comes from the kids around school, but when the adults give me praise, it feels a little wrong. Mrs. Daye returns to her crossword. I wait to take a few sips, counting the seconds to ask for Christi.

"Where's Christi?"

"Of course, Jester, Sweetie," Mrs. Daye replies. "She and her little brother are in the back doing one of their little films." She gives a wink. "I'm sure she'd be glad to see ya."

"Thanks."

I leave the family room and can't help staring at the walls of the staircase decorated in a collage of family pictures. I look at Christi, and even when she was younger one can tell she was going be great. Not many families in Ashton have lives such as the Dayes'. They're not rich, they're not poor; they're just a family. One of the only few functioning families we have left.

I head through the dining room to the kitchen and pass a fully set table with a basket full of bread and a side of butter set in the middle. Next to each empty plate is a small salad covered in dressing. My mouth waters at the smell of a cooking roast as I approach the back door. Through the window I see a vast, empty backyard blanketed in snow. I open the door, the chill hits my face, and a child-like squeal screeches, "Hey! Watch it man! You're messing up my shot!"

"Easy, Hoppy, you better watch that temper. You never know who you're gonna be yelling at," I say.

He takes his eye off a camera phone, looks up, and jumps. "Whoa, Jester! Sorry, sir! I didn't know that was you!"

He drops his head.

I lift his chin.

"Shut it, Hoppy. Just giving ya a hard time. Where's your sister at?"

He lifts his arm and points to a massive tree stripped of its pine. The entire trunk is bare, except for a line of offsetting branches reaching towards the top like a crooked ladder, and at its peak sits Christi with her board teetering over the top limb.

"Christi! What the hell are you doing?"

A faint whisper crawls down the tree. "Jester? Is that you? What did you say?"

My body, in a cold sweat, suffers from frantic beats. I scream, "Get down! You're going to kill yourself!"

Another whisper crawls down again. "Get down? You want me to get down?"

"YES! NOW!"

"Okay."

The spotlight from Hoppy's phone presents wisps of falling snow from a pitch-black night. Repeated sounds of cracking and crunching branches build like distant thunder, and once she reaches the light, I'm struck. Branch by branch, she uses both sides of her board to maintain balance and form, landing on a curved sheet of ice to divert her falling force. She bursts towards us and shouts happily, "Watch out!"

I try to catch her, but she barrels me into the snow. Holding me tight, she giggles on the inside of my chest, rolls over, and gives an adrenaline-fused sigh.

"That was awwwwesome!"

As we hold tight, I can feel her breathing and the sensation is one I want to last forever. Without a word, she caresses her upper lip to mine, and I forget the cold. Life is forgotten. Until Hoppy squeaks in. "Ewwwww... gross. Mom, Dad, Christi is kissing Jester!"

With a furious whisper, she says, "Shut up, Hoppy! Go inside!"

He puts his head down, turns, and under his breath, mutters, "Fine... still gross."

She releases her boots from the board and turns to me. Her eyes beam. She holds the delicious tension for a perfect amount of time.

"Hi."

"Hi," I repeat. How are you this fine evening?"

With a kiss to one neck, then the other, she finishes with a third on the tip of my nose and says, "Well, it's nice now that you're here." Again, her lips caress mine and we roll together, using the snow as a blanket.

After some of the best minutes of my life, she scrambles off me, grabs my hand to hoist me up and says, "C'mon... it's cold. Dinner's almost ready. I want to watch the end of the game too."

But I stop her.

"Wait... Christi. We need... I mean, I need... to talk to you about something."

She draws back.

"What? What do you mean?"

I pull her back down next to me.

"Look… I promise, it's not bad. I'm all in for us. So remember that I said that, before I have the next thing to say."

"Okay."

I bring her hands to my lips and gaze into her eyes.

"I… I need you… we need you to represent us in the Chute."

She steps back in a furious bolt. She cries angry tears and screams, "What?! What the hell do you mean? Why me?"

"Christi, you're all we have left."

She turns away, shakes her head, hands on her hips.

"Is that what all this was? You were just using me?"

I pull her shoulder to face me, but she torques it out of my hands.

"I know it may look that way, Christi, but it's not. I wish things could be different. I'm sleepless thinking about ways things could be different."

"Different? People die in the Chute!"

"Don't you think I know! Kids have died in the past. If there was anyone else I could ask I would, but there's not. You, Christi, you're the only one that can save us."

"I can't." She looks down with the fury gone. "I… I… I've never done anything like that. I'm afraid."

"Christmas, I'm responsible for Ashton. I was born to it." I point to the kitchen window at her parents and two siblings preparing dinner. "See that, Christi? That's a family. No one has a family anymore. At least, not one like that. You're one of the last ones. Your life is a life that people don't even know how to dream about. My friends, kids from school, Ashtonians and I, don't get to experience what you have, Christi. Look at your life."

Her eyes tear up. She takes a deep breath and says, "The Chute, though! I've never ridden down a mountain before. You really think I can do it?"

"Think? I just saw you jump down a 50-foot tree. You're crazy, girl. That's why, I lo-… like you."

What the hell just came out of my mouth.

"Let's just get to dinner," she says.

I try to give a gentle kiss to the top of her forehead, but she moves away.

It was a nice invitation, but I have no idea what to do at the table. I look at the silverware in front of me clueless as to which one to use. July notices and mimics using the salad fork.

Thank you, July.

I try not to embarrass myself throughout the meal. Even her parents feel the tension, and we eat in silence looking at each other across the table with awkward smiles. Christi is emotionless.

Dinner is cold. Not the food. Christi doesn't say a word. She doesn't eat much and after what seems like hours, she stares at the plate and moves a pea back and forth with her fork.

The torture ends. I do the only things I know and help wash the dishes. Using the same gallon of water, the Dayes are careful when it comes to cleaning the dishes because they don't have enough water. Her dad made their money years ago as a Denver Bronco. Mrs. Daye fills the sink with soapy suds. After the final plate, I exit the kitchen and Christi is waiting for me at the door. I make a last attempt before leaving the house and in a whisper I hold her wrist. I pull her within inches and say, "But seriously, think if you *do* win. It doesn't just help us. The whole world gets a chance to see you. No more blurred internet videos. The real deal."

She walks a few steps shuffling in the snow. Silence.

"I'll make sure you have everything you need. "

She pauses and then kisses me on my cheek.

"Okay. I'll do it."

"Really? That's amazing!" I pick her up and spin her around and around. "I believe in you, Christi. We're—I'm so lucky to have *you.*"

She jabs a friendly punch to my chest.

"Shut up, J. We're lucky to have you."

After a few quiet moments, I text Benny and before Christi and I say goodnight, he arrives with Irish's limo. I say, "There's one more thing."

"What?"

"What would you say to being Queen?"

"Queen? Me? What about Vivian? Why?"

"You don't have to do anything. I'll explain later. Just practice winning the Chute."

I get down on one knee, bow my head, and kiss the back of her hand. So what do you say, "Would you be my Queen?"

She smacks me on the back of my head. "Shut up, weirdo. I don't know what you're up to, but yes, it would be my honor."

19.

QUEEN OF THE HILL

POWDER MATCH: 18 DAYS

A COUPLE DAYS LATER, Christi and I sit on a porch swing in front of her house, waiting for Irish to pick us up to meet the Brigade. "J., I don't know if I can do this," Christi says.

I brush her cheek with my thumb, raise her hands, and give her a soft kiss.

"I know you can. I promise. I'll be there the entire time. Nothing bad will happen."

"The Chute is one thing, but being Queen is another. What if—"

"No 'what ifs.' Just do what we practiced and everything will be fine. Just remember, it's all in the eyes. Look directly through them."

Her hands tremble.

"You'll be there with me?"

"Of course."

I'll never let you get hurt.

Benny pulls up in the limo. I open the door for Christi and the limo lights turn on. Rose and Irish are sitting on the side behind Benny as we get in. Rose is already talking.

"Hey! So you're the Christmas Daye everyone in school has been talking about," she says. "I've only seen a few of your videos. Those goggles don't do you any good. You're fine, girl."

"Videos?" Christi says. "Oh, yeah. The ones my brother posts. I haven't seen any. Thanks, though."

Rose's voice sharpens. "No, I'm serious! How the hell do you do that? Jumping off buildings, scaling walls, jumping off trees... don't you get scared?"

"Um, not really. It's just fun, I guess."

Rose leans forward facing Christi, while Christi broods, her hands in her lap.

"Fun? You kidding me? That looks terrifying! If that's fun for you, I don't even want to know what makes you scared... you always this quiet?"

We stop at a red light, and I glance to Christi's anxious eyes and try to send her a smile.

Christi says, "I'm sorry. I don't mean to be quiet, it's just my first time going to the Hill. And honestly, meeting the Irish. Thank you for this opportunity, sir."

Irish nods.

"Sir? Christi honey, don't call him sir. After tonight, people will be kneeling before you." She massages the back of Irish's neck saying, "Plus, he's just a big softy."

A smile escapes through a crease of his mouth. He pulls Rose in close to kiss her on her forehead.

Rose scoots next to Christi and says, "I'm sorry. I'm just excited. I'm Rose Punch. It's nice to meet you."

She reaches her hand out for a welcoming shake. Christi shakes her hand and takes a deep sigh of relief.

"Thank god," she says, blowing a wisp of hair from her forehead. "Punch? I've heard that before. I remember you from the first day of school. What Vivian did was terrible. She's awful. I sent a 10."

Rose presses both hands to her chest and says, "Christi! Thanks for seeing things my way."

"No worries. I've always hated that demeaning rating in the Hall. I still hate it. I like your style, your presence."

Rose laughs and says, "Ha! You liked the nerdy chic look. No wonder you and Jester get along."

"Shut it, Rose," I say.

Christi gives a delicate laugh.

Rose says, "Ah! There's the Christmas I've been looking for. These guys are so damn serious. It's nice to have a cool girl around. You want to hear a secret?"

They lean in together, but I can still hear everything.

"When I first met your man over there, I saw a *Playboy* on his desk." With one hand. She makes a stroking motion.

Christi covers her mouth and giggles.

"Like one of the old ones. Where there's way too much down *there*, if you know what I'm saying."

Christi shouts a laugh.

My face heats. "Shut it, Rose! Dammit."

"Easy J., geez. We're just having girl talk here. Every man has his preferences."

Irish laughs this time.

I shout, "Those aren't my preferences! I mean… just shut up. We're almost at the Hill. It's almost time."

As we approach the last curl of road, an orange glow swirls into a cloudless sky of stars. The engine stops. Irish steps out of the car and opens the back door for Rose. Before she leaves, Rose reaches into her purse as she leans to whisper something to Christi. Irish opens the door for her and they leave Christi and I alone in the limo.

"Christi? Is everything okay? You ready?" I ask.

All I can see is the top of her white Queen hood. She doesn't respond.

"Christi? Christi? CHRISTI?" I ask.

Nothing.

I look down to her lap. She's holding something. Petting something. But I can't see it. I jump out of the car and enter the back alongside her. I place my hand on her shoulder. I reach for her chin to see her eyes, but she turns to the window.

"Christmas, what's wrong?"

"Nothing."

As I look to her lap, the night sky illuminates a fuzz of white hair. I realize it's the polar bear. I take her hand and together we stroke the bear's fur.

I tell her, "Christi, you can do this. We know you can."

She takes the bear from my hands and scrambles out of the limo. I jump out to catch her, but she continues walking forward.

A blinking orange-yellow hue breaks through a forest of trees. We approach a fire made of twigs and wood stolen from model homes. Trailing Christi, we approach the flame. Rose, Irish, Curly, and Mars sit huddled over the embers with bottles of water for the fire. Once Christi approaches, all four stand, pull their hoods, and bow their heads. She sits down on an empty log next to Irish with Rose on his left. She keeps her eyes on the bear; I sit next to her to rub her back. She doesn't protest.

Okay. The fellas are in. Now, all we need is Shea. You can do it, Christi.

I scope out the circle. Our eyes converge. Irish looks to me. I look at Mars. Mars looks to Curly. He checks his phone, looks back to me, and rubs his hands back and forth. Mars stands, stretching his arms across his chest, while both Irish and Rose crack their knuckles. I roll my neck. We wait.

Christi interrupts the silence. "What's it like?"

"What?" I respond.

She looks at her hands and asks again, "What's it like?" This time looking at Irish.

All eyes dart around the fire.

"What's 'what' like?" he says and the air is swallowed around us.

"Being the Irish."

I move to apologize, but he interrupts.

"Hopeless."

"That's sad."

He sniffs the cold air.

Her fingers quiver.

"Aren't you scared? Like of the brawl and stuff?"

The fire pops. Cracks. Pops.

"Ashes are death, Christmas. If we're already dead, then why be afraid of dying," he says grimly.

"I guess you're right. It's just…"

"Just what?" he snaps.

She doesn't back away at his coarse tone and continues. "It's just sad. You're still a teenager, a kid like us, even though we tend to play grownup, ya know."

He locks eyes with hers. "Being a kid is a luxury I don't have. I lost my family years ago. Ashton is the only family I have left."

Rose kisses him on the cheek.

Christi says, "Even though I still think it's sad, I just wanted to say thank you."

"Thank me after you win," Irish says.

"I'll try."

"Christmas… you need to do better than that to convince me. The only way you're beating Sonny is to be fearless."

Rose chimes in, "Geez, you two. Take a breath. Just like Christmas said, 'we're kids.' Let's have some fun."

The calm is interrupted by a flash of a match in the darkness from the bottom of the Hill. Gentle wisps of bent grass and broken twigs precede Shea as he approaches the circle with a reaper hood masking his face. I place a hand on Curly's shoulder, and he flicks the cig stick into the fire. He unzips a collar at the bottom of his nose and pulls the hood from the top of his head.

Shea. We need Christmas. Just listen.

"What's going on?" Shea asks.

I tell him the plan.

He's hesitant. Shea glares at Irish and walks towards us.

I whisper, "Christi, it's time. Become our Queen."

Her body trembles, but she doesn't hesitate to look up at Shea. They challenge each other upon meeting; a tear drops from her left eye, but she doesn't blink.

He demands, "Answer me! Christmas! Do you know what this means?"

Christi's strong, but I don't know if she can handle all this pressure. She's been snowboarding years for fun, but being Queen and taking down Sonny is another level of commitment. But, she knows she needs Shea to get us to that slope.

She keeps her eyes on him.

An abrupt wind ruffles the fire, almost putting it out, but the flames flare again. Christi stands tall looking down at him.

She kneels. She holds his hand to her heart and says, "Yes, Shea, I do." She fights against her tears to speak and brushes oily locks of hair from his coal eyes.

"Shea... it's me, Christi. We grew up together. Remember when we snuck out into the woods, and I got my foot stuck between two rocks, and we were attacked by a bear and you saved me by throwing cheese at it. But in the end, it was just a racoon?"

Damn. Even I didn't know about that.

He laugh-cries with a snort, throws himself in her arms. "I'm so sorry, Christi! I wasn't thinking! It's just..."

She holds his head to her chest, rubbing his back, saying, "Shh... Shh... it's okay Shea... don't worry... it's okay... everything's okay. Everyone's scared."

He pulls himself back, and asks her with an innocent tone, "So, is it true? You'll win, Christmas? We won't have to deal with the Cherries anymore?"

If Christi and I win, we won't even have to fight in the Snow Brawl.

Christi stands him up. She looks to Irish, he stands, and we follow. "Shea, I can win, but I need your help."

She's even sexier when she's confident.

He pulls back. "My help? With what?"

"I can win the obstacles in the Chute, but I've never been on a mountain slope. If we find a slope can you get me there? Without the Cherries knowing? I need a mountain, Shea. You're the only one that can get it."

"And if I do, you'll win?"

She smiles. "You bet I'll win."

Shea looks to Christmas, his eyes brimming with hope. Then he looks around at all of us with a grin and says, "What the hell are you guys doing? This is our Queen! Get her a drink or something."

He winks at Christi. "Sorry, Madame Daye. It's an honor. I'm at your service."

He picks up a carton of beers and throws it at both Curly and Mars, then rolls laughing down the Hill. Irish and Rose laugh at them and stay back with Christi and me.

I grab Christi's hand. Moonlight shoots between a small-cloud opening and the only thing we see is a bunch of kids tumbling down a hill, laughing. I look to Christi. She looks at me, but holds out the bear for a me to kiss it on the nose and hands it back to Irish. She kisses me on the cheek. Together, we look down. Together, we roll.

20.

WELCOMING THE NERDS

POWDER MATCH: 15 DAYS

I T'S MONDAY MORNING.
A delicate tinkling of an alarm bell wakes me. I try to find my phone, but it's hidden in the morning gloom. I look to the clock next to my bed. It's 6:30. I still have five minutes.

I hug my pillow and turn over, but my phone rings. I search around my bed through an ocean of blankets and can't find the damn thing. As I reach for my bed-lamp, the ding repeats with a vibrate under my ass. When I grasp the phone, I read a string of texts.

6:20—Irish: I'm here.

6:22—Irish: You Ready?

6:24—Irish: Where you at?

6:25—Irish: C'mon man...

6:27—Irish: of all days dude, seriously?!

6:30—Irish: If you don't answer, I'm breaking the door!

Eyes still blurry, I rush through my pass code, but screw up the first few attempts. A car door slams. I regain sight, press the code, and call him. "Yo...," I say.

"What the hell man? I said, 6:40. You ready?" Irish asks.

"No! I'm not ready. Damn, man, breathe. I'll be down in a few."

My street is lit in a bruised blue hue cast by a late falling moon. It's starting to snow. I enter his limo. Instead of smoke and stale booze, I'm overcome by the musk of an old man's cologne. It's like he took a shower in it. Almost choking before I spit out a question, I look to Irish, stunned. His hood is pulled back. He has gelled hair. His facial hair is mostly shaven with a few dry bits of blood.

His shirt is too tight. His pants are too short, showing strands of tape he uses to hold his socks to his shins. He's washed mud from his duck boots. I laugh.

This must be what he thinks "dressing nice" means.

"What are you doing?" I ask.

He slaps my arm and says, "Shut up, J.! I've never done this before."

It's just the Academic kids.

"Done what?"

"You know…" He looks in the rearview mirror and licks two fingers to flatten his eyebrows. "Look respectable."

"This is you looking respectable?"

"I need practice."

He reaches in his pocket and finds his lighter. After a few attempts, he lights a limp cig stick. He inhales.

I say, "You know, man, the Academic kids are just as nervous as you."

"I'm not nervous," he says.

Yes, you are. Maybe not nervous, but excited.

He takes another puff.

"You know these kids?"

"From the Academic Hall? I know only a few. I have an idea who Rose picked."

"Good… 'cuz I'm never waking up this early again."

"Ha… me neither."

Leaving the limo, we run to the school through a blizzard, enter through the doors, and brush off snow from our hoodies. The gentle taps of isolated steps through a soulless Hall is actually calming. Each Quarter bench seems asleep as we pass. As we turn left, the Academic Hall is lit in yellow light. A wisp of light reflects along the brick floor from the auditorium door. Before we enter, we're stopped and forced to turn around. It's Ms. Madonna.

"Ms. Madonna? What are you doing here?"

She moves between us and unlocks the doors.

"Shhh… don't tell anyone. Rose told me your plan, and I am in for anything that makes this school better. Good luck." We can hear a few whispers behind the door, but as Ms. Madonna opens it, silence takes over. Irish allows me to enter first, and follows.

The stage is lit with spotlights, focused on five figures, their heads held low. Rose leans against the front of the stage, legs crossed. She hands me a large bag filled with fresh Quarter-minion hoodies, kisses Irish, bows, and heads back to her position against the stage. I look to Irish for a signal. His eyes remain on Rose and he nods for me to begin.

"Welcome," I say. "I'm sure Rose has filled you in on the request of The Irish and The People of Ashton for your services. However, before we can proceed, we must confirm that your skills are of use to us. This is our last chance, though. The world will see your skills."

"Water," a voice crawls from the line.

It's Brick Ball, a kid I know is brilliant from class, but an ass. He raises his head and nods with subtle obligation.

He spits on the floor and rubs it away with a sneaker. Through massive glasses, he looks to me, then holds his eyes on Irish and says, "Our families need water."

"I'm sure with your math skills you can figure that out without us," I respond.

"Well, I want to win. Prove to everyone that Ashton is more than just drunks and losers. There's still hope in Ashton. I'm the best in math and physics you're going to find."

"Prove it," Irish says.

After a heavy sigh, he rolls his eyes and commands, "Say any number with 4 digits."

I call out, "2,222."

"Now a number with seven digits," he says.

"2,222,221."

"Give any other number."

"222."

Brick starts. "2,222 multiplied by 2,222,221, divided by 222 is exactly 22,242,230. Good enough, sir?"

I check my phone's calculator. He's correct. Irish reaches in the bag, shuffles around, and throws him a red hood. "How'd you do that?" I ask.

Irish commands, "Brick Ball, you're a part of Five-Points now. You know what that means, right? Whatever Mars needs, you get it done."

He snatches the hood off the floor, snatches a water from Rose, and sneers, "Yes, sir."

Nobody moves.

Rose slams down the rest of Irish's 24-rack of fresh water.

"Okay then... one... state your name... family... show your skill," Rose says.

A small, coal-eyed kid with smoky grey hair raises his head, wrestling his hands together. He takes three deep breaths before beginning to speak. Quiet, yet confident, he says, "My name is Spark Heater. My dad runs the furnace at the factory. I'm... I'm... not good at things. I don't read good. I don't speak good. I don't do math good either."

Irish elbows me and gives me a confused look. Having never met the kid, I look to Irish and shrug.

"That's okay, man... Spark, is it? What can you do?" I ask.

He chokes his hands. He looks to Rose. She gives him an assuring flick of the wrist.

"I'm good at fire," he states.

"Fire? Like making a fire?" I ask.

Spark begins to giggle, but catches himself and says, "Sorry sir, anyone can build a fire. I can manipulate it."

"Manipulate?"

He looks again to Rose, she nods, goes backstage, and pulls out a small table with a tapestry, waxed wires, a slingshot, and two bowls, one filled with white powder, the other filled with kindergarten shapes in a transparent bowl. Raising one finger, he says "Give me one minute."

Rose pulls out a phone, sets the countdown timer to sixty seconds, and says, "One, two... go."

In the first 15 seconds, he stretches the wire across the table and places the tapestry on top and spreads the powder.

Before the 20-second mark hits, he moves the bowl of shapes to the edge of the table. He holds lighters with both hands and ignites both sides of the wire. Sparks fly an inch a second. He waits.

As the sparks reach the middle, he grabs the cloth by each corner. A white flash explodes. He pulls the fabric in opposite directions, creating a majestic canvas of white smoke. Then, one by one, he shoots each shape from the slingshot through the canvas of smoke, making the face of a jack-o'-lantern.

Awed, I look to Irish and with a reciprocal look, he mouths, "That was kinda cool."

I turn back and the kid stands alone with a strand of dying smoke around him. "Spark, is it?" I ask.

"Yes, sir."

"That was pretty cool."

"Thank you, sir."

"If you don't mind me asking… what's in that wire? I've never seen fire like this before."

His hands wrestle. "With all due respect it's a family secret. We were the first furnace keepers for the factory."

"Don't worry, man, just asking. If you had the material, how much wire could you make?"

"Any size, sir. With the right amount, I could light up the entire valley."

Irish reaches into the bag and tosses a grey hoodie at his feet. "You're now a Smoke, Spark. That's your Quarter. Rose will give you the instructions."

Spark picks up his gift, bows his head, and walks off the stage.

Harp Skye, who got shamed in the Gauntlet, paces on the stage. She walks into a spotlight. She sings, "Old Devil Moon" from the Broadway musical *Finian's Rainbow*. I can tell she's been on stage before. Half-way through the song, Irish throws a black Freshmore hoodie to her feet.

The next kid sits on the floor, arms crossed, with a beige hoodie shredded along its brim. Face unseen, he sucks on the pull strings like a pacifier. Irish elbows me to speak. Rose appears from behind the stage. Knowing who it is, I look to her, she looks to me, and nods.

What is Twitch doing here?

"Twitch, is that you?" I ask.

His right shoulder jolts, but he remains still. His youthful face stares at the floor, emotionless. He acts like he doesn't know us.

He's getting worse. What are you doing, Rose?

I shrug at Irish and before I can speak to Rose, she's already walking towards Twitch. Holding her hands out, she reveals the polar bear, kneels to his eye level, and whispers in his ear.

He raises his hood and caresses the bear's soft, white hair and brushes it like the mane of a stallion.

Damn. Who knew that stuffed polar bear would come in handy?

Rose lets him brush it once more and pulls it away. He reaches for it, but she pulls it back and says, "Twitch, I know you love the polar bear. We all do. But it needs you to do something for us."

She looks to me. I look to Irish. He looks to her.

"Twitch, can you help us?" Rose asks.

The strings of his hood drop from his mouth as he nods his head in assurance.

Rose pulls a paper and pencil from her backpack and places it in front him. With the polar bear in hand, she raises Twitch's eyes to hers and says, "We need a perfect picture of this in two minutes. Can you do that?"

His left shoulder shudders. He doesn't respond. She crouches close to his face and asks, "Can I trust you with this, Twitch?"

Twitch wrenches his fingers, and reaches for the bear, but she pulls it back. He cowers.

God he's bad. Twitch would never cower. The Cherries will do anything to win.

"Twitch, we need you. Can I trust you to protect him, if I let it stay with you?"

His eyes widen as he reaches for it like a drug fiend. She pulls back.

"We need that picture, Twitch," she says.

He picks up the paper, throws it in the trash, and runs behind the stage. Within seconds he re-enters with a block of molding clay from the mask room. He places it in front of her and raises two fingers. She asks, "Two?"

He creates a circle with his arms.

"Two? Circles? Two spheres? Two cycles?"

He slams his head in frustration. He jumps off the stage, grabs the piece of crumpled paper, and draws a sun and moon.

"Oh... two days? You want two days with it?"

He claps his hands smiling.

"Well, I don't know, Twitch, this is very important to Irish and me. Is there a way you can show us you can take care of him?"

He jumps and points to the watch on Rose's arm and raises five fingers.

"Five minutes?"

He nods, "Yes."

"Show us, Twitch," Rose says.

In less than four minutes, using nothing but the blunt pencil, saliva, and his own hands, he sculpts a figure of the polar bear in perfection.

Damn. That's sick. I mean he did something similar last year in the Powder Match, but damn.

"Wow!" Rose says. But before she hands him the toy, Irish throws a grey hoodie at his feet. I look to him. He whispers to me, "Make sure Twitch is protected."

The academic kids exit, leaving one person alone standing on the stage.

Mixy Kombow. Her family has been creating our Sweet concoctions for the Cherries for years. Those concoctions help us lose the Powder Match. While it's not Mixy's fault, she's been made an outcast. Irish stands, turns his back, and leaves the room. With her head down, she waits for the door to open. When it shuts, she raises her head to me. Mixy is small, brunette, and more beautiful than sexy. She stands before me vulnerable and alone.

"What are you doing here, Mixy?" I ask.

She grips the back of her neck and says, "I want to help."

"*Us*, Mixy? You want to help us win?"

She lifts her hand from her neck, looks down, holds both hands together. Pleading, she looks to me and says, "I just..."

"You just what?

"My parents are sick, Jester. I know why you, why everyone hates my family. They, we, didn't ask to be the chemists. I... I may not know what it's like to watch my parents lose their minds to alcohol, but I do have a glimpse of what our family used to be, and what it's like to come home to love. They don't love anymore. They're numb, J. They don't even talk."

135

I feel a little of her pain, but stay strong and say, "I'm gonna need more than that, Mixy. It's not just me. Everyone knows the "special" Sweets from the factory come from your parents. Those asshole Cherries throw it in our faces every chance they get."

She takes a deep, saddened breath and confirms, "I know."

I feel sorry for her a little and say, "Okay… so let's say we do give you a chance. What can you do?"

She gathers herself, opens her eyes, and says, "Well, it's not easy to say, it's easier to show."

My phone beeps with the message from Rose saying: **We're ready.**

The time underneath her message shows 7:55. I look to Mixy. Her eyes respond with a hope for a chance. I take a few seconds to think. "You have ten minutes. The Hall is yours, in ten minutes."

Leaving her alone on stage, I hear a whisper of a "thank you" as I head out the doors. I turn left to the Academic Hall and meet Rose with the new Quarter minions waiting to enter the Activities Hall. Each wearing their proper hood, they stand in line, heads bowed to the floor.

I place my hand on each shoulder and say, "No matter what you think, or how you feel about your worth, understand this: you're our heroes now. Those hoodies are not gifts. You have a responsibility. You walk like royalty. Do you understand me?"

More reluctant than expected, they raise their heads, look to each other, to Rose, finishing with me. I walk over to Rose, shake her hand, press a gentle kiss on her cheek, release and open my palm towards the Hall.

Rose turns and heads in the opposite direction. Twitch runs after her.

She heads back to him, embraces his face with both palms to look him in the eyes and says, "The bear is yours now. As long as you have him, you have me. I'm right behind ya."

She kisses Twitch on the forehead and leaves. He falls back in line, clenching the toy to his chest.

The noise from the Hall is different as we reach the corner before turning. It's not quiet, it's not loud. It's waiting. I take a deep breath, look back, see the academic kids' eyes cloaked in fresh hoods. They follow me in to the Hall.

Well, this should be interesting.

Like successive waves, each Quarter stands at each step as we walk past, presenting ourselves to the entire Hall. We line up perpendicular to Irish and the Q1's.

Vivian, trying to capture a selfie, takes a few moments to recognize the entire Hall standing with hoods and heads down, hands behind their backs.

"What the shit?" she scolds.

She looks to Irish.

He stands tall and turns towards her.

"What the hell is going on?"

He doesn't respond.

She storms towards me, stabs a finger into my chest, and says, "What the hell is this, Jester? What are these losers doing in here? I want to know right now!"

I pinch her finger, pull it away from my chest, and say, "Vivian, you're officially relieved of your title. You're no longer Queen of the Hall."

Startled, her voice shakes.

"What? What do you mean? How? Why? We had a… a deal." She turns to Irish. He looks back to her, eyes cold.

I reach for her shoulder. She jolts back with demon eyes, and speaks to me in a slow, burning tone. "Then who is the next? That bitch, Rose?"

Irish jerks towards us. I raise my hand to stop him. She heaves like a stabbed animal as I respond as calmly as possible. "Vivian, this is about Ashton and hope. You're still one of us. Still a Q1 Chicklet. We've come to the consensus that Ashton would be best represented in this year's Powder Match by someone else. Sonny has gotten bigger and better. We need someone better too."

Vivian's face is frozen in shock, and there is a slight bit of panic in her voice. She responds, "If not that Rose girl, then who?"

"Chris—

"Christmas Daye is to be *my* Queen," Irish says.

21.

KINDLING

Drawing back in fury, Vivian snaps a look to Christi sharp enough to jolt the Hall. Arms rigid and fists clenched, she storms towards the Five-Points Quarter. Christi stands still and strong. The Cousins stand behind her.

Vivian's eyes dart as she clenches her lips and points a finger towards her, screaming, "You dirty little, back-stabbing whore!" She swings an open hand, but Christi catches her wrist before it hits. She tries a clumsy left, but Christi grabs her other wrist and pushes her away.

Christi says, her voice steely with resolve, "Look, Vivian, this wasn't my idea." She presses her finger into Vivian's chest and says, "My job is to win the Chute. You bring your personal issues up with Jester."

Vivian's face turns beet red. Her expression isn't one of anger but embarrassment. Her chin quivers. Tears well in her eyes and smear make-up down her cheeks.

"Screw him. Screw all of you!" she shrieks. "I'm getting the hell out of here. Let's go, Chirp."

The Hall stares at Chirp.

You're not her side-chick anymore. Stand up for yourself, Chirp.

Head down, Chirp crawls from her spot on the bench and slinks down the Hall, until Christi stops her.

"Don't take another step, Chirp."

Her head lifts in confusion.

"Don't listen to that bitch. Chirp, you're mine," Vivian warns.

"No one owns you. Not now," Christi responds. "Not any more. If anything, you're a needed friend. I'm going to need some help with all this."

In a last ditch attempt, Vivian demands, "Let's go Chirp... now, dammit!"

This time, she doesn't move.

"Chirp?"

Chirp clops her heels together and stands straight with her head up in defiance.

"I think I'm going to stay, Vivian."

With a defeated, strained voice, Vivian asks, "What? But... I thought we were friends."

She searches the Q1 bench for support from her Chicklets. They look at their phones.

How does it feel, Vivian?

I open my hands and press my palms downward to bring myself an inner peace, "Look, Vivian, this is our chance to take Powder Valley back. You're still welcome; still a Q1. The world needs to see Christmas beat Sonny. Queen beat King. We're tired of merely surviving. It's time for the Ashes to rise again."

For a moment, I see a glimmer of a fresh tear swell from Vivian's eye. Before it falls, she swipes it away before turning on her heels to leave. She storms out, slamming the door as she leaves. The Hall sits waiting for any movement, until Chirp walks up to Christmas, takes her hand, and guides her to the Q1 bench.

Every kid pulls up a hood in respect. Christi arrives at the Q1 bench. Chirp releases her grip and presents Christi to Irish and me. "Your Queen."

Christi looks at me. I wink to her and raise my own hood. She turns to Irish. With a gentle grin, he kneels, grabs her hand, kisses it, and presents her to the Queen's chair.

Chirp goes next to her, and sits down. The Hall is frozen in awe.

Chirp whispers in her ear and Christmas covers her mouth in embarrassment and eventually says, "Sorry, everyone, you can sit now."

Hoodies pull forward and the tension vanishes. Excitement and relief ignite the Hall.

Letting things settle for a bit, I give some time for Christi to adjust. I send a text to Mixy to ask if she's ready.

I text: **You ready?**

Mixy: :)

As Mixy enters the Hall, a loud "What the hell is that bitch doing here?!" explodes from the Five-Points Quarter.

The entire Quarter stands, throwing crumples of foil, plastic wraps, and empty cig stick packs at Mixy as she enters, hands behind her back.

Mars tries to quiet them down, but the raucous shouting makes his attempts futile. The rest of the Quarters follow as Mixy approaches the center of the Hall. She looks to me. I look to Irish, then Christi. Her grin turns quick and straight as she stands to confront the room. Curly's Quarter goes silent and the rest of the Hall follows in contagion.

A different Christi speaks. Not speaks, commands: "I know that many people in this room hold anger towards Mixy and her family. Even I will affirm my own disdain for the misdeeds brought upon Ashton. However, in this day of challenge, we must change to prevail. We cannot blame her for the mistakes of her ancestors. Nor can we allow her abilities to go to waste.

"Irish, Jester, and I have agreed to give Mixy one chance, to show all of us, not only what she has to offer to Ashton, but also a chance for redemption, for acceptance. In the future, I will be open to discussion on any matter, but this matter is not negotiable."

She sits down, then stands back up and says, "Oh, and one more thing: no more scoring and that stupid Gauntlet ends today."

Good job, Christi.

She looks to me nervously, and I nod to her proudly. She sits down, faces the Hall, and commands, "Mixy, the Hall is yours."

Mixy says, "Thank you, Queen Daye."

Out of her left back pocket she pulls out a plastic bag of tobacco and rolling papers. Out of the right, she pulls a smaller plastic bag of blue powder. She mixes the two together and rolls a Spliff.

She walks over to Curly's bench, reaches to Twitch, and pulls him over with a delicate curl of her forefinger. She asks the Hall for a lighter.

No one moves.

"Please."

No one moves.

Irish tosses his lighter at her feet. She places the Spliff in her mouth, attempts to light it, but fails.

No one moves.

Twitch takes the Spliff himself, and lights it in one try.

What's she doing? What's he doing? What's in the Spliff?

The Hall stares at his every move. After a few preparatory puffs, he inhales, and blows a plume of blue vapor towards the arched ceiling. Chin up, he gazes at the smoke until it unfolds. Once it dissipates, the *real* Twitch speaks. He's ignited. Even I'm caught off at the sound of his voice... like a ghost.

"Why the hell is it so goddam quiet in this house? Geez, it's awkward in here."

He looks at Irish and with a smirk, he says, "You loser."

Holy shit. He's back.

He arches his back, stretches his shoulders, and with both hands jolts his head to crack his neck. He pulls off a hood and dirty blonde hair sprouts in different directions, but he looks good. Healthy. Handsome even.

Irish wipes a tear when seeing his brother, and asks, "Twitch? Is that you? I mean... the real you?"

"You bet your ass it's me."

Mixy, you're a genius. It's Twitch. The real Twitch.

Twitch addresses the rest of the Hall with open arms and declares, "I want you all to know that I am the one man in this part of the valley that has ever knocked out The Irish."

The Hall waves in murmurs until Twitch clarifies by saying, "Granted, he was asleep and had no idea what was going on, but it still counts... haha." He turns back to Irish and me. "How you assholes been doing?"

I respond, "Where you been, Twitch?"

He reaches his hand out for a shake and pulls me in for a hug, whispering to me, "I don't know how much time I got, but it's good to see you guys again."

He heads to Curly, stops in front of him, and says, "Well, look who it is, good ol' Curly Brown."

In a little shock, Curly responds, "S'up? Twitch, how you been, bruh?"

"Good, man. Thanks for taking me into your Quarter. I know I'm a little different now."

Curly laughs.

"Ha, no worries, dude, Smoke's missed ya, bruh." He slaps his shoulder and says, "Just make sure you keep smoking that."

Seriously, Mixy, how much of that do you have?

"I'll see what I can do," Twitch says.

He heads to the Five-Points Quarter and says, "Mars, I love you, man. You know I'd die for you. But, I'll be honest, I'd kill for a date with your sister."

Fighting a smile, Mars comes back with, "Damn, man, I hate that I love ya. It's good to see you around these parts."

He heads back to Mixy and gives her a massive hug, whispers something I can't hear, but I know it's "Thanks."

Twitch addresses the Hall again.

"You should be ashamed. Mixy is family. And this is how you treat her?"

Circling the Hall, he states, "We die. Cherries live. That's been the rule. Her family is keeping us alive by giving them their freakin' drugs. If you're looking for a hero, it's her."

He points to Irish. "I love you, man. I'm always here. I can't wait to take them Cherries down together."

He kisses Mixy on the cheek.

Irish unzips his personal hoodie and reveals nothing but a torn, blood-beaten, white t-shirt. He places the hoodie around Mixy's shoulders.

I knew the academic kids could help, but bringing back Twitch can save us. She deserves to be a Q1.

The minute bell rings.

No one moves.

Random texts of confusion blast through my phone throughout classes. Not bad, mostly a bunch of "WTF's!"

22.

AT THE BRIDGE

POWDER MATCH: 11 DAYS

O N FRIDAY, THERE'S A booming party inside the Bridge. When we step into the Bridge after school, it's as if Ashton has been reignited.

Every Quarter is drinking together as if they were a colony of best friends. Music blasting, drinks flowing, even the Chicklets are trying to teach Twitch how to dance. The world is different and scary, but better.

Thank you, Rose.

Irish and I wait for Christi to sit down. Under the table, our fingers weave together.

Christi squeezes my hand. Nudging her shoulder down, I slide to her cheek and say, "This is your town now. Go have some fun."

I can't help smiling at the site of her joining her new Chicklets on the dance floor with Twitch.

Twitch was always a player.

The floor is flooded with sloppy drunk dancing.

I open my palm and invite her to the floor, and together we dance with the rest of the family. Minutes pass like seconds. We laugh together like we were kids again.

Curly and Mars lean together with arms hung over each other, confessing their brotherly love.

Irish and Rose arrive with their hands entwined. She looks to me and gives a soft wink and a smile as Christmas kisses my cheek.

I smirk to show my thanks.

Irish then forwards me a text from Rose.

Rose: **How'd it go???**

He looks to me for help. I take the phone from his hand and I respond for him.

Irish: **Good.**

Next, the sound is so loud, I send him my own text.

Jester: **Dude... c'mon man. She's yours! You don't need me anymore... ha.**

Irish: **Ha... true, true... thanks man!**

Irish: **Hate to be a buzz kill... heard from Shea yet?**

I'm interrupted mid-text by a delayed message from Shea.

Shea: **Vivian's in Cherry Ridge.**

The bar door slams open. The party dies. Murdered by reality, Shea tumbles through the entrance. After catching his breath, Shea tells Irish, "There's a boat outside. Near the lake. I can't carry them in."

"Them?" Irish asks.

He storms out the room and minutes later, Irish drags a small boat carrying two bodies. He falls, exhausted. Mars and Curly catch him.

"Clove!" Rose screams.

I demand, "Everybody out, now!" Curly and Mars send out their Quarters. Christmas sends the Chicklets. Rose takes Twitch with her.

In terrified shock, Curly and Mars come to the boat and pull out the unconscious bodies. It's Clove. They pull him off, and beneath him lies Vivian, bruised, scarred, and covered in melted wax. She's somewhere between incoherent and unconscious. Her eyes are pinpoints and her skin ice cold. She's been drugged! Irish leads Shea to the bar.

"Mars!" I yell. "Take them to the hospital. Keep him breathing."

I turn to Christmas.

"You need to get out of here, you don't need to see this."

She pulls back in defiance and walks towards Shea. I grab her arm, she pulls away, and says, "I'm the Queen. I'm staying."

When we reach Shea, he's trembling. We both rub his back. I nod for a few shots to Seamus. Shea's hands are frigid and brittle like shattered ice. I pull them apart and place the shot between them.

"What the hell happened, man?" I ask.

He doesn't respond. I look to Christmas. "We got to get them to the hospital," she says to me. I whisper to Shea, "Come on, Shea, just tell us. You're home now."

"Did you hear me?" Christi asks sternly.

"Yes."

"Irish, get Benny. Take them to the hospital," Christi commands.

Irish and Benny drag the boat to the limo.

Christi, Shea, and I are left alone.

"Was it Sonny?" I ask.

Shea says, "For sure. Their parents let them do anything."

Tears flow from his bloodshot eyes. Christmas holds him.

"It's okay, Shea," she whispers. "Not much more. I promise. Just try, for me." She grabs a napkin off the bar and wipes his nose and cheeks.

He starts: "I was just making sure the path to Clove's was clear for Christmas. Clove's green light was blinking on the end of the dock. I tied up my canoe and crept past Sonny's house. I heard a sound. I walked around back and saw a white light on a tree trunk next to me.

"I followed the light back to the house. I couldn't see much. Then I saw her. Vivian… inside the house, hanging from a hook like… like a drugged scarecrow. I have no idea why she was there.

Maybe to make a deal. Dammit, Vivian. Never trust Cherries.

"Anyways, I moved around to the front of the house. I saw an ancient disco ball through the window. The kids were passed out.

"I thought they were too drugged to notice. I broke the window and I waited. Nothing happened, so I went in. I crawled over a valley of dollars, pill cans, and nitrous shooters. I grabbed Vivian and carried her to the window. I placed her on the floor and thought it was safe. That's when I heard a yell.

"I turned back and saw Sonny standing in a doorway. I picked up Vivian, jumped out the window, and carried her through the woods to the boat. I heard sirens. I saw lights everywhere. I thought I was caught. That's when I heard Clove."

"Clove? What was he doing there?" I ask.

He looks at me and slaps my arm. "I know, man. Sonny must have had him out on town alert or something. Clove was panicking."

"Then he jumped on top of us and he shoved the boat off the shore. We got hit by rubber bullets.

He winces, but pulls off his hoodie and presents blood-bruised blisters forming massive lumps on his back. Shea holds his forehead with his two blue hands. "But somehow we all got out of there. Clove saved us."

I look to Christmas.

She embraces Shea and kisses the top of his head. She sways him like a baby, pulls away, looks him in the face, and assures him, "It's over, Shea. They're done. I'll make sure of it."

She looks to me and says, "Take care of him, get him right, and get me that mountain. No more games. It's time to show them the real Queen."

23.

CLOVE

POWDER MATCH: 10 DAYS

Clove wakes up the next morning in St. Patrick's Hospital, shocked, angry, and scared. "What the hell? Where am I? Where's my mom? What the hell happened?"

I press both palms to his chest, lay him down on the bed, and say, "You're fine, Clove. You're both safe."

"Where's my mom? Where is she?"

I point next to a sleeping Vivian and show him his mother sleeping peacefully next to her. "She's right there."

Groggy, lost, and confused, he asks, "What? I don't understand. How did you get Mom out, J.?"

"It was a part of a plan to get you back to Jimmy and Rose."

"I don't understand," Clove says.

Rose enters the room between the Cousins. Clove sees her, looks at their mom, and the past six years of pain hits him all at once.

Rose and him hold each other crying.

Clove says, "Our mom is sick. We never should have moved to Cherry Ridge."

"We got some Sweets to help with the pain," Rose says.

"The Cherries could have saved her. Mom can barely open her eyes."

147

I'm sorry, Clove. I'm sorry, Rose.

Rose says, "You know, Clove, Dad has always said that our mother was his lucky charm."

Clove says, "Well, luck is a combination of skill and planning. I just want to see those Cherries go down."

He looks at Irish and me. "So this Christmas girl can beat Sonny?"

How does he know about Christi? Word in this valley travels fast.

"With practice," Irish says.

Clove wipes his eyes, stands up, and shakes my hand.

"I want to meet her. Where is this Queen?"

24.

GREEN LIGHT

POWDER MATCH: 9 DAYS

THE NEXT EVENING, the air bites my face as we cross the Cherry side of Powder Lake. Our boat is more of a box on water. It only fits four and needs power strokes to move. Thank god we have Irish.

Irish works both oars. Shea directs us across the moonlit lake. Huddled together, Christi and I fight for breaths of warmth. The boat is silent as it weaves through broken ice sheets. The silence is palpable. We wait for Clove's signal. A green light flashes at the end of his dock. It's Clove's truck.

After we beach the boat, we climb into Clove's truck. It's electric and quiet. He takes us up a side road to the top of the mountain. We drop Christi off at the slope's peak.

Christi is the only one of us who isn't afraid. We wait for her at the bottom.

She's got this.

Christi heads down the mountain, turns and weaves, but falls. Rooster tails of snow catch the moonlight. Each fall feels like a broken plate sounding against the floor. Attempt after attempt, Christi's falls turn to pain. The mountain is sliced in broken crescents. Powder snowboarding is much different than street snowboarding.

We're screwed.

I get a surprising text from Vivian and present it to Irish.

Vivian: **It's Chirp. I'm using Vivian's phone. Vivian wanted to pass this message. She doesn't have feeling in her fingers yet. Damn, Cherries. She wanted to say to Christmas, "You can't beat Sonny at his own game. You have to surprise him."**

Christi sits with gloves over her face in the middle of a massive pit of snow. Half-way up the slope, I can tell she's crying.

I yell at Christi, "Vivian sent a message. I think she wants to help. You should read it."

Her head shoots up.

She must be desperate to take Vivian's advice.

She bee-lines down the mountain and is next to us in a matter of seconds. I show her the text and ask, "What does she mean, Christi?"

Christi eyes the mountain and the single line she just carved in the snow.

"I know exactly what she means," she says.

PART III.

THE POWDER MATCH

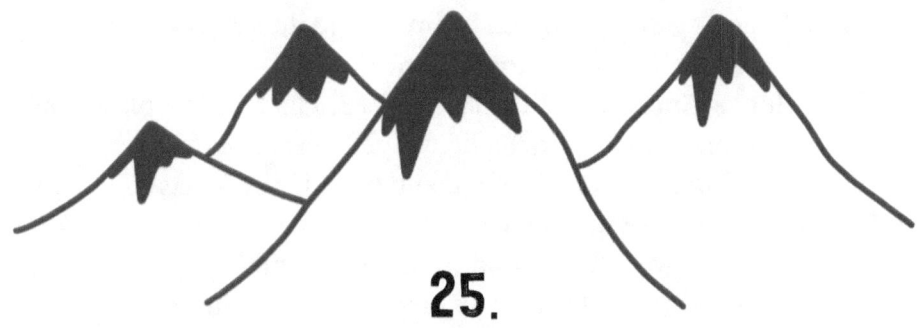

25.

ACADEMIA
IN THE GYM

POWDER MATCH: 00:15:00

IT'S 6:45 P.M.
Mixy, Twitch, Harp, Brick, and I sit around the locker room. We sit with a bit of confidence as we listen to the broadcast.

In fifteen minutes, the world is going to watch as we compete for our livelihood. The Academia Trials aren't just a test or science experiment. Each category is a presentation of applied intelligence. Anyone can be smart, but using intelligence is different.

The clock reads 6:50. Inside the Ash gym's locker room, an old flat screen glitches with sputtering visuals. Three judges appear on screen. A small, stocky man, with smoky grey hair, speaks with a voice deeper than a ship's horn. His suit is grey and subdued. It's one of the Powder Match announcers, Rex Specter. Rex's voice comes through the speakers.

Rex: "Hello, America and the rest of the world watching! We welcome our 100 million viewers to the annual three-day Powder Match between the Ashes of Ashton and the Cherries of Cherry Ridge. I'm

Rex Specter and again, I'm joined by my tele-mate, Cherry great, Barry Pine. How are you doing, my good friend?"

Barry looks almost twice the size of Rex. His face is a plastic surgery A+ example, and his mocha hair is gelled into perfect waves. His suit screams a highlighted mix of red and blue. He even has a matching bow tie, pocket square, and shoes.

Barry: "Doing well, Rex. Good to be back home."

Rex: "It's always good to see you. Before we begin, just a quick recap of the rich history of these games. Ashton won the Powder Match years ago and that's when the videos struck the internet. After millions of followers, the competition grew. Ashton lost one of its greatest champions, Jimmy "Irish" Punch, leaving the power of the valley to his so-called Jester, Jay Connelly. Not much later, Connelly lost his life in a tragic car accident, leaving the entire valley in the hands of the youngest Ashes in history. His son Jeremiah and his best friend Reginald "Irish" Slay have emerged as the leaders to face the Cherries."

Barry: "I knew the old Irish. Ashes are good people, deserving of a good moral leader, and he was just not that. While I remain impartial to whoever wins, I can attest that the Cherry Ridge way of life is always a good life, and our Ashton brothers do not have the same experience in Powder Valley.

Yeah right, prick.

Rex: "That tragic story always gets me, Barry, but you never know in the games. We will just have to see what the Ashes have left. They do have an interesting ace up their sleeve."

Barry: "And that is?"

Rex: "The Ashes have made a change for their Chute competitor and Queen!"

Barry: "What? No one told me."

Rex: "Queen Christmas Daye. Her videos first popped up on the internet when she was only three. As a toddler, she was jumping off buildings onto railings for fun. As the years progressed, her stunts became mythical."

Barry: "Honestly, when I saw her fall from the very tip of a Redwood, transition to a grind across two trees, I thought it was a hologram. Since then, I found out she is for real."

Rex: "Rumors came about that she was no phantom, but she remained hidden within the bowels of Ashton."

Barry: "How did they convince her to do this, Rex?"

Rex: "They didn't. She volunteered."

Barry: "Volunteered?"

Rex: "As we all know, Ashes keep things very close to the heart and rarely communicate with the outside world. My sources say Cherry Ridge's Sonny Gatson is bigger and stronger than ever. The Ashes knew they needed to make a change. Once they submitted their list of competitors and her name showed up, more than ten million people worldwide subscribed to a pay-per-view package of the games. Even I have caught the Ashton spirit."

Rex puts on a tailored suit-jacket with a hood.

Barry attempts to look impartial.

Barry: "Yes. We see. But before we head to the Chute. It's time for the Academia portion."

Rex: "That's right! Again for the new viewers, could you enlighten us on the Academia rules?"

Barry: "Each town enters five contestants, 18 and younger. We will start with Applied Physics, followed by Music. The next events are Chemistry and Art. The culminating event is a test of Literature. The Ashes will be fully stacked for the competition. In previous years, it has just been a couple kids from Ashton. This year they will have specialists in each category."

The clock advances to 6:55.

The locker room door opens. Christi, Irish, Rose and the Cousins enter.

Christi sits next to me with the Cousins behind her. Irish stands in the middle with Rose. I look up to him. "What's up, man?" I ask.

Rose steps forward and one by one she presents new hoods especially made for this portion of the games. Crimson silk with gold thread.

These are sick.

Christi says, "Vivian asked me to give you these. The Ashes are known for their intelligence. If the world's going to be watching, they deserve to see how great we really are."

The scene on the screen cuts outside to the streets of Ashton.

Barry: "And here come the Cherries."

Escorted by an entourage of Berries is a trail of five sleek, glossy, red, white, and blue hover-limos. As they near the gym's entrance, it looks like they're heading into a war zone. They mean business.

Barry: "Still gives me chills."

Rex: "It is quite a sight. And here they come through the smoke of Ashton. Just in time for a commercial break."

We enter the gym and our side is filled with teachers and even our principal, Mr. Sweeney. The gym is swamped with red, green, black, and white hoods except for a small square patch in the right corner for the Cherries to sit. We take our seats to the right of the judges' table. Rex and Barry sit atop in the left corner. A massive tele-screen remains blacked out on the center wall as we wait. It switches back on as the Cherry hover-limos pull up. A few Berries open the doors of the first four limos. Out of each limo exits one silk-suited Cherry boy, or Barbie-esque Cherry girl in a satin cocktail dress.

Rex: "We're back. Wow… glamorous and breathtaking are the only words to describe the sheer beauty of Cherry children."

Barry: "Couldn't have said it better myself."

The gym doors open and the Cherries enter, marching in precise formation and sit down, crossing their legs in unison. Sonny sits with two of his snow maidens. They stand and the audience follows in mutual respect. Before they sit, the snow maidens open a wooden chest to present a rare polar bear fleece blanket on the bleachers for the Cherry Royals to sit.

They act like we're the same. The world thinks we're the same. We're not.

Jimmy Punch, his wife Jameson is in her wheelchair and Mom, are joined by Rose and Clove. Rex and Barry's voices boom through the speakers to introduce the beginning of the Academia competition.

Rex: "Welcome, all, to the first chapter of the Powder Match called Academia. Five events: Applied Mathematics, Music, Chemistry, Art, and Literature. Best of five wins."

Barry: "I know that compared to the Chute and Snow Brawl this part of the competition may seem boring but, let me tell you, this is not just a battle of nerds. It's a battle of the best minds our wonderful nation has to offer."

Rex: "That's right! Before we begin, though, we must show the world the woman they've been waiting to see. The Lady of Honor, The Snow Queen, New Queen Christmas Daye."

Christi enters wearing an immaculate pearl-white hood. Irish and the Cousins are at her side as she approaches the Cherry Royals, Daisy and Sonny.

Christi kisses them on both cheeks along with an obligatory hug. The Cousins present him small boxes in each hand containing Euphora-Sweets. Sonny accepts and sits down after Christi and Irish take their seats behind our bench.

Rex: "All right, here we go! First up, Applied Mathematics. What is the challenge this year, Barry?"

Barry: "Well, the rules are five minutes for planning and five minutes for production. The challenge for Applied Mathematics this year is a throwback to years ago. It involves the old plastic pieces from the Lego company.

Legos?

Rex: "Lego?"

Barry: "It was just a building toy at first, they even made movies about it back in the day. Mathematically, depending on the size and shape of each piece, it's the epitome of physics. The only part of the challenge is that each piece must be used. Then the judges will determine the winner based on the final display."

The center screen presents a display of a Lego piece.

Rex: "That doesn't seem too hard."

Barry: "Wait. Just you wait."

The judges enter.

Rex: "I guess we'll just have to see. Who are the competitors?"

Barry: "Five Cherries against Brick Ball."

Rex: "Brick Ball? That's an odd name."

Barry: "His family designed the Sugar Sweet factory years ago. One of the best mathematicians in the nation at the age of eight, he is another surprise entry in the lineup. If he wins, it would be a great start, considering they always have their Jester in the end. Jeremiah Connelly, or Jester as they call him, has won the literature portion easily in past years. If the Ashes can somehow make it to him, then an upset is ever possible."

Rex: "All right everybody, you heard him. Cherries up first. Put the five-minute prep clock on the board."

The Cherries spread into three groups, huddling together.

Rex: "What are they doing?"

Barry: "They split into math, physics, and visual display. Brick is going to be tough to beat."

The prep clock ends. All five huddle together to create their piece. From a narrow view, we can barely see anything, so all we do is watch the clock tick to the very last second.

Once the clock chimes, the Cherries present their compilation. They unveil a pristine green, grey, purple, and orange display of a Pikes Peak sunset.

Barry: "Geez, is that a display or the real thing?"

Rex: "It certainly is impressive. The judges act as if the display was expected. Predictable, you think?"

Barry: You could be right. I'd like to see what Brick Ball can do alone.

Rex: The judges are waiting as well. Let's find out.

Brick approaches the center of the gym. He lifts his red hood and waits for the prep clock. It sounds.

He picks up buckets of small, medium, and large grey, black, and white plastic bricks. After a minute, he slams the buzzer to stop the prep timer. The judges whisper among themselves. He waits for the 30-second break for the performance clock. It sounds.

He begins. Like watching a video game nerd, he builds with precision large brick to small brick. Colors blend into a three-dimensional, ten-foot display of Snowdrop Peak. With only the white bricks left, and in a circular motion, he maneuvers around the summit. A shoelace falls over the brim of his shoe, and he slips and tumbles down with only 30 seconds remaining. Gasps roll through the walls of the gym as he races to the top to finish. In the final seconds, he drops his final white cube to finish the peak of the mountain and raises his hands in expectation of the crowd to follow, but he's met with disappointed eyes.

Searching around below, he realizes that a small black cube has broken off on his fall to the wood floor. He climbs down and crawls to Christi in shame. He pulls his hood over, eyes in apology, and leaves the gym.

Dammit, Brick. It's not your fault. We still have Twitch, Mixy, and Harp. All we need is two wins. I'll take care of the rest.

Rex: "Ouch! I wish I had the words. What a masterpiece! It's sad to see a competition end with a technicality."

Barry: "True, true, sometimes bigger isn't better."

Rex: "Guess so. Well, the Cherries have taken a surprise first win. What's up next?"

Barry: "Music. Nothing complicated with this one. It's all about who sounds better."

Harp tries her best, but being so young and inexperienced, she chokes up on some high notes. The Cherries play like an orchestra and in a few words… we are slaughtered.

Shit. Well, no room for mistakes now.

Rex: "That was painful."

Barry: "Always a tough one to win for the Ashes. Not really known for romance."

Rex: "The Cherries are now up two. The Ashes must win the last three to become Academia champs."

Barry: "This will be interesting. The Ashes have their big guns coming out. Mixy is the daughter of the chemists of the Sugar Sweet factory."

Rex: "Seriously? Some of their concoctions have been known to cure dementia, Alzheimer's, and in some cases, brain cancer."

Barry: "This one will be very tough for the Cherries to win."

Mixy stands in the middle of the gym with a table filled with components, waiting for the prep clock to begin. Sonny stands and speaks for the Cherries. He says, "We *concede* the chemistry portion."

Huh? Concede?

Rex: "Whoa."

Barry: "I'm stumped."

Sonny must not want the world to see her talents.

Mixy walks to the bench, confused. When she sits, I place a hand on her shoulder and tell her, "They're afraid of what you could show the world. There's nothing you could have done. It's an easy win and we need you for Twitch."

Rex: "Here comes the Art portion. The score is 2-1, in favor of the Cherries."

The Cherries send out a single vixen. A girl I've never seen before. Perfection in human form, she spends all ten minutes using four brushes clutched between of her fingers to create a photographic re-creation of Michelangelo's *David*. I'm stunned, and for the first time a little concerned about winning the competition. She sits down with an arrogant smile.

Twitch walks up, Rose's bear in hand, and Mixy follows.

Rex: "It's Twitch Slay. A surprise entry considering he was really damaged in last year's Snow Brawl."

Barry: "Didn't expect to see him... he's like Lazarus."

Mixy pulls out a blunt, much larger than the Spliff in the Hall, places it in his mouth, and lights it with Irish's lighter before walking to the bench. Just before Twitch blows out his plume, she lifts her hood, looks to Sonny, and gives him a look of death, followed by a subtle middle-finger.

Twitch's back is turned to the audience. He stands next to a table with a 3x3-foot wide piece of clay and a box of similar size made of sugar glass. A booming beat fills the air and Twitch nods to the music. The prep clock ticks down and Twitch walks to each part of the gym, creating a wave of dancing fanatics. He runs around the gym one final time to create a fluid wave before the prep clock runs out.

With his back turned, he hides his creation from all of us. Wheeling, dealing, cutting, and scraping with a scalpel, his arms move in controlled chaos. The only thing we can see is the crowd whispering in shock and awe.

He finishes with a minute and a half remaining. He places the black sugar glass over the piece, turns to us, lights a cig stick, and waits as the clock ticks. He pulls out the scalpel, taps the glass, it shatters, and when his piece appears, I'm stunned. It's a miniature duplicate of Michelangelo's *David*. He finishes by placing the lit stick in the figured hand, lifts his hood off, and gives a threatening glare to the Cherries. The crowd roars. Twitch wins!

Next, Sonny enters to try to beat me.

Rex: "The Ashes have struggled with Academia in the past years, but their strongest contestant, Jeremiah Connelly, has won the Literature portion three years in a row."

I'm going to win. I don't lose in Literature.

The first questions are a breeze. Some of my answers include Mary Shelley, Ayn Rand, Edith Wharton, Mark Twain, Ernest Hemingway, F. Scott Fitzgerald, and Suzanne Collins.

The final question is a tie-breaker: What Irish-American author ran for Governor of New York in 2006?

Yes! *Angela's Ashes* is one of my favorite books. "Frank McCourt!" I yell.

Bing!

Am I wrong?

Sonny answers: "Malachy McCourt." The brother of Frank McCourt.

A hushed silence covers the gym. He's right. I'm wrong. Academia goes to the Cherries.

Shit, I failed. I failed?

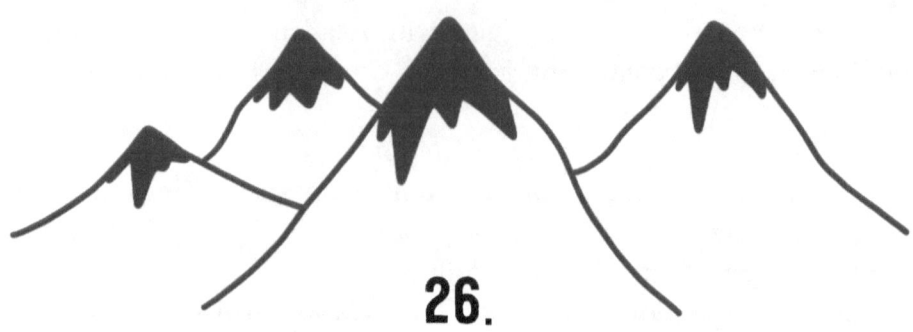

26.

BRINGING IT HOME

MY STOMACH ACHES and a panic attack strikes as I walk to the limo, Christi runs after me. She grabs my arm and I snap back with a fist, but realize it's her and restrain myself.

"What happened in there?" she asks.

"Get the door, Benny."

I get in and she attempts to follow. I push her away and say, "I'll text you."

Shea gets in the limo after me. I can't control my anger. I pound the nearest whiskey bottle and throw it at Benny's window. I almost hit him. "What the hell, man?" he asks.

"Take me to the Hill, Benny." I command.

For the first time, I see a timid Shea who says, "Maybe we should take a second to breathe; calm down a bit."

"Calm down! Calm down! Do you understand what the hell just happened?"

"I… I mean a little?"

The last thing I remember is yelling at Benny to leave me at the Hill.

A slap on my back wakes me up on top of the Hill. I swing a fist and it's caught in mid-air by, to my surprise, Irish. I look to my right and see Christi lying next to me in a thermo-bag. I slam my fist to my palm, challenging Irish.

"Guys!" she cries out. She slaps my face and yells, "He's here for you, J.!"

"What the hell are you talking about? I ruined everything. For all of us." I say.

I get up and walk a few feet towards a rare rising sun. I put my head down.

Christi and Irish approach behind me from both sides. Irish's hand is on my shoulder. "Shit, guys," I say. "Now we have to go back on the Snow Brawl pitch. And it's because of me." Irish whispers in my ear. "It sucks you lost man, but I am kind of glad we get a chance against those Cherry pricks."

Trying to twist emotion and reality together with my hangover looming, I ask, "What's next?"

Irish picks me up and throws me off the top of the Hill. I roll a few times, gather myself, and see Rose, Jimmy, Clove, Jameson, Twitch, Curly, Mars, Benny, and the Cousins.

"What is this?" I ask.

Rose speaks loudly: "We're family, J. We live together. We die together. Till the end." She pulls her hood and raises a fist.

Christi grabs my hand, and Irish my shoulder. He says, "Let's take this valley back, brother.

27.

THE CHUTE
CHRISTMAS FIREWORKS

I T'S 6:45 P.M.
The limo is full and weighs heavy in silent tension as Benny drives with Shea up front. Irish sits with one arm around Rose and the other tapping ash outside the window. Butter, Scotch, and Clove occupy the side-seats, while Curly and Mars sit across from them. Christmas, fully suited in an inky black snowsuit, goggles on top of a glossy black helmet, sits still but her calm is betrayed by a nervous twitching leg. While I'm consumed by everything in the Powder Match, I know the only thing on her mind is the Chute and that's all that matters.

As we roll up the plateau of the Dam, Cherry Ridge and the Snowdrop Resort illuminate the valley like an old-time amusement park. Red, white, and blue searchlights stream above the valley as if searching for fallen American heroes in the sky. Fireworks crack and boom from surrounding Cherry mansions celebrating the ceremonial opening of the Chute. Upon approach following a loud explosion, Christi shouts, "Stop the car!"

Everyone jumps and Irish slams the driver's window to stop.

"Is everything all right?" I ask.

Christi takes a bottle of infused water from the limo fridge, swigs a massive gulp, coughs, and finishes saying, "I'm fine. What the hell is the matter with all of you? You're freaking me out! It's not like we're driving to my funeral."

I brush a braided lock of hair behind the back of her neck and touch her twitching leg. "We just figured you wanted some time to focus."

She smacks my arm. "Focus? I've had two weeks' practice on Clove's slope to focus. I got this. It's not like I haven't seen the Chute before."

Everyone looks at each other; I look at her with a smile.

Curly says, "Finally… thank god… I've been waiting to light up." Mars passes a blunt and then pours a shot for each person. Everyone raises their glass and Rose says a few words: "From those who were born to die to those who were born to live, go screw yourselves." She raises her glass to Christi and says, "Christmas, go pop those Cherries."

Christi claps her hands once. "Let's do this."

We blast music in the limo, roll to the end of the Dam, and glide through a gap in the barricade. This the only time we get to use their roads. They're grey, pristine, and perfect. I remember being amazed by these mansions, but they make me sick now.

Bottle rockets and firecrackers fly and blast in every direction.

When we arrive at the The Snowdrop base, the village is lit in blinding white light. Lining the front of stores, crowds of Cherries stand with hoods pulled over their heads to mock us. The limo stops, and so does our music. Irish presses a side button on the door, and a four-sided holographic television rises from the floor of the limo. The voices of Rex Specter and Barry Pine carry through the limo.

Cheers charge through the background of their mics.

Rex: "And here he is, the reigning King of Cherry Ridge and Powder Valley, Sonny Gatson, looking almost twice the size as the last time we saw him. Look at that!"

Barry: "Wow! Yes! I remember when he was a freshman. Now, he looks like he could break me in half."

The cameras transition from Rex and Barry to Sonny's slope-side deck. Exiting the doors, he appears on the railing like an emperor addressing his subjects. He wears a sleek white snowsuit, designed to hug his body like paint. Marlboro-red C's decorate both sides of his gleaming royal-blue helmet. Golden locks flow from under the back of the helmet. He pulls down his goggles. They shine with a white, golden tint. Two snow maidens bend to buckle his boots to his snowboard. Once he's ready, and from a standstill, he leaps to land perfectly balanced on the bannister.

He slides down the railing of his spiraling steps to the slope, sweeps six inches of freshly fallen powder with palms open, and lands. Flowers from every family shower over him. He takes both his helmet and goggles off, throws his head back, shaking his golden mane, and blows a few kisses, making both the girls and women scream. He ends his display with an arrogant bow while holding one arm straight out to the side.

Dammit. That was a good entrance. Sonny knows what he's doing.

Back in the limo, Curly jokes, "Gross."

We chuckle for a second, but once the cameras turn towards us, tension fills the air.

Rose interjects, "Butter… Scotch… take care of her."

Christi grips my hand and kisses me. The doors open and the Cousins exit, standing firmly in front of the door. The feed still playing in the background, Christi exits. The doors close.

Outside the limo, Christi stands with her hood down. Butter carries her board, Scotch her boots. She taps both on the shoulders and they take their first steps into the village.

As they approach the village, Cherries, lined across the storefronts, pull over their mock-hoods and after her every step, throwing black roses to molded lettuce, they shower her and the Cousins. Young Cherries sneak through the crowds to spit Cherry pits, one even bold enough to attempt to reach Christi, but Butter and Scotch shove him back into the crowd. They turn the corner, and the street of heated brick is steaming and now free of snow and ice. The Cousins sweep away the dead flowers with their feet as she approaches the Snowdrop base.

Rex: "For our new viewers, especially those tuning in to see Christmas Daye, could you give a brief overview of the rules for the Chute?"

Barry: "Sure, Rex. Actually, it's pretty basic. It's a race down the mountain. Whoever has the best time wins. An expert boarder can complete the course in under two minutes. Starting at the peak of Snowdrop, both riders slide down a pitch-black slope of unpredictable terrain, the only lights coming from the helicopters attempting to maintain a visual of the two competitors. Once through the "Black Hole," as some call it, each rider must board through "The Tube," and finally a climactic "Chute" in which each rider has one jump to display in front of the judges in case of a tie. As they race through the Chute, each rider must collect signature emblems from their respective towns. Roses for Cherries and Sweets for Ashes."

Rex: "And what is the significance of the emblems?"

Barry: "Cherry Ridge is known worldwide for their botanical creations, while Ashton is famous for their concoctions of Sweets from the Sugar Sweet Factory."

A helicopter settles at the Snowdrop base and the judges exit.

Cameras pan to the inside of the gondola where Sonny sits relaxed and confident with one leg up on a seat.

The Cousins separate, place Christi's boots and board in the gondola, and present her to the judges: three professional snow boarders. She bows in respect. She turns to the gondola, picks up her boots, and enters. The door slides shut behind her. Both cameras and sound turn to the inside. She sits opposite Sonny. Leg still up, he sits, chewing on the stem of a massive clover, and starts the conversation.

"Christmas, is it? So, you're the new Queen who everyone's been boasting about. You're Jester's girl, right?"

Christmas remains still.

Sonny says, "Figures he'd pick a mute. He never shuts up. How is Coffin Corner, by the way?"

"I live in Ashton," Christi says before they both grow quiet on the trip up the mountain.

A silence carries the two up the mountain.

A miniature version of Snowdrop is presented three-dimensionally through the tele-screen in our limo. The cameras zoom into Christi and Sonny's gondola. The gondola stops and the doors open; Sonny opens his palm flashing the clover, and allows Christi to exit first.

His show is impressive. He looks like a nice guy. Who wouldn't root for chivalry?

Christi stands, opens up her palm, and says, "Life before death."

Sonny flicks the clover at Christi's face.

They grab their boards and buckle up atop Snowdrop Peak. Cameras out, only audio is left.

Sonny speaks. "I can beat my best time in my sleep. Good luck."

Christi says, "Luck? The Irish don't need luck. They're born with it."

Back in The Limo, Mars says, "Damn J., Christmas is hardcore."

Irish and Rose respond together. "Seriously."

Curly finishes. "I felt bad saying, 'damn,' around her, but hell, she's got bigger balls than I do. Is there something you're not telling us, J.?"

"Shut it, Curly."

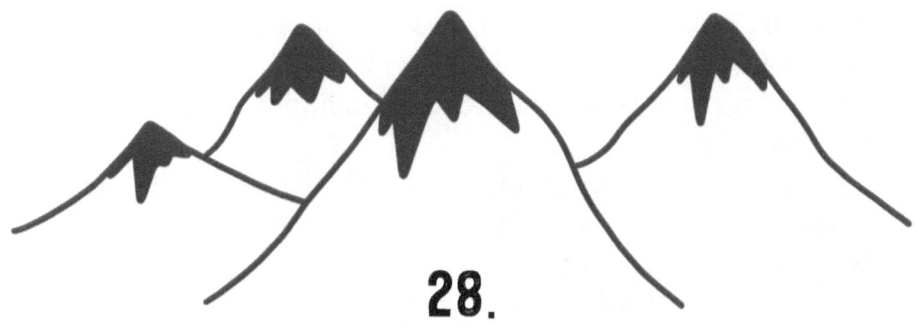

28.

CHERRY BLIZZARD

THE HELICOPTER VIEW shoots in and the alarm sounds. With a little light from the moon, Sonny darts back and forth down the peak. He burns through the powder. Seconds pass, and the cameras catch his entrance. Fans scream as he takes a sharp cut right into the famous Ice Tube. He winds up and down through a family of Aspen trees and skates like a bobsled. He approaches the exit, circles upside down to grab the emblematic rose from the ceiling of the Tube, and lands switched.

As if it's nothing, he approaches a massive oak and shreds pounds of snow to stop at its base inches before impact.

He heads down towards the Chute and tucks to maximize velocity. He approaches the final jump with a massive explosion of white, red, and blue rose petals. He bursts through, pulls two backflips with a final upside-down 360-degree helicopter spin and finishes in perfection. The time clock shows 59.30 seconds.

Shit. That was fast.

He takes a smooth, wide turn, and Cherries present him with more showers of fresh flowers. He slows to a crawl in presentation for the judges, pulls off his helmet, waves to his fans, and places the three roses in each vase. His hair is strewn about from the harsh wind. His skin is flushed as he heaves in quick breaths, smiling. In front of the final judge, he holds his hand up for the crowd to quiet and bows.

You can do this Christi. C'mon, Sweetie. You can do this!

Rose asks, "Can? Did Christi see his time?"

"No," Clove says. "Once they reach the summit, all she can see are a few lights from the village."

Rose asks me, "Is Spark ready?"

"Yup… as long as the Cousins get to their points, we're good to go."

She bites her nails.

The Heli-cams pan to an aerial view of Christi.

Rex: "Well, the door is wide open for Christmas Daye to steal the win, but she's going to have to beat Sonny's new record. Let's see if the rumors are true."

Clouds dissipate and the Heli-lights present Christi standing, breaking in both sides of the board to warm up. She jumps a 360-degree turn to start her run.

Rex: "Well, this is new."

Christi heads straight down the mountain. She leans on her back leg, pulls the front board up, and snowboards through the powder.

Barry: "This girl is fearless."

Snow sprays in waves as she gains speed. The Heli-lights can't keep pace. Cameras zoom to her gloves and show Christi grabbing the first bubble-gum sized Sweet as she enters the Tube like a bullet. She exits with two Sweets. In a flash, she bursts through the Tube toward the oak tree. The crowd gasps at her pace, waiting for a deathly impact. Just before she hits the tree, she jumps, pounds the tree perpendicular with her board, and snow falls like sugar on her back as she stomps the landing. Using another 360 swoosh for speed, she shreds shaved ice for show. As she exits, she crouches, holding both knees to gain as much speed as possible in readiness for the Chute. She collects the third Sweet.

Upon her incline, a whisper comes from Irish: "C'mon girl."

The cameras jump cut to the center and in a moment, Spark's line appears at the base of the Chute. A wide-angle shot shows both Butter and Scotch holding the end of a rope. The rope ignites and they pull together. A thick, pure white cloud blankets the view of the peak, blinding the tele-screen. Silence takes over. A small circular figure breaks through the white wall of smoke.

170

She rolls two flips and creates a single smoke ring that floats upward into the atmosphere. As she finishes with her own helicopter, she lands identical to Sonny's presentation. The breathless crowd watches her drop the Sweets next to each rose in the vases. She stands next to Sonny. She unzips her coat, revealing a deep grey, tight, voluminous blouse. She reaches inside her cleavage and pulls out Sonny's clover. She leans in Sonny's direction and drops the clover along with the Sweet in the third vase and says, "Child's play."

The clock shows 59:00 seconds.

She did it! I love you, Christmas Daye.

Rex: "She did it! Ladies and gentleman, Christmas Daye has won the Chute. Anything to add, Barry. Barry?

Barry: …

Rex: Barry is speechless. Christmas Daye is the winner. The Ashton Ashes have tied the Cherries of Cherry Ridge. Join us tomorrow for the explosive final event, the Snow Brawl.

I burst out the limo's doors. Snowdrop is dead quiet.

Lines of people are still standing, heads down in silence. Curly and Mars swerve back and forth through each alley spread wide like gliding eagles. Irish picks me up, places me on his shoulders like a toddler, and we burst upon the base in elation. Silence has overcome the valley to the point that snowflakes hiss as they land on the pavement.

Christi, still, almost frightened or in shock, turns and runs towards us. I pat Irish to let me down. Not a moment after I land, she tackles me to the ground.

In my right ear, she whispers and asks, "I did it, J. I did it!"

I say, "Sweetie… you killed it."

The Cousins pull her off me and place her on their shoulders. Irish picks me up along with Christi. We run together through the village. Heads still down, Cherries present a cig stick or an Irish clover in respect. Curly and Mars collect as many as they can before we reach the limo. Rose awaits with her hood down. When we arrive we all align our hoods. We turn back to the village, bow in respect, and get inside.

This is awesome! Christi has given us a chance to win. Tomorrow, the Snow Brawl begins.

We blast the same music we came in on. Windows, seats, glasses, and drinks shake at every beat. Rose pulls a bag from her side and hands each one of us a chilled, large bottle.

Christi exclaims, "Champagne!"

Once she pops the cork, a shower of foaming, sugar liquid sprays all over me. Blinded, I wipe the liquid off my face. I take mine and shake and shoot it at Irish. The entire limo turns into a champagne suds fight. Irish wets a bundle of towels and tosses them to all of us. We dry off. Rose offers me a glass of champagne.

I want so much to enjoy this and take a sip. I want so much to drink. But I want Christi more.

Christi takes a sip of her own glass and says, "It's okay, J., I'm not your mom."

No. You're better.

"Seriously, guys, it's fine. I got a big day tomorrow, anyways," I say.

For the first time, I watch people around me drink. It's nice to observe hope and happiness.

We head towards Ashton and hear booming sounds. Clouds shine in bursts like watching a lightning and thunderstorm from up above. After years of despair, Ashton is filled with life. Rose opens the moon roof from inside the limo and says, "Get up there, guys. Your people want to see you."

Christi looks to me, I shrug, she takes my hand, and pulls me through the roof. We ride through the streets. Families of two, three, or even eight are standing and cheering, throwing their only Sweets in celebration. Christi weeps in my arms. I kiss her and say in her ear, "It's okay, Sweetie, most of these families think they're dying. Sometimes hope, or even the chance at life, is better than any medicine." I raise her head from my chest and she kisses me. Her tears are the sweetest things I've ever tasted.

Finally, sitting down in the limo, we get a chance to breathe and let the adrenaline settle. Once we sit, Christi jumps on top of me, overpowering me with a heavy, tongue-filled kiss, and then jumps off.

"Get it girl," Rose jokes.

"I feel amazing!" Christi screams. "Better than any trick ever!"

Irish says, "Couldn't have said it better." Underneath the seat, he pulls out a case with 24 bottles of water and hands it to Christi. "For you, Christi. Bridge, anyone?"

Christi stares in awe. No one ever receives such a gift from Irish. She's speechless.

"That was insane!" Curly says.

Mars says, "Seriously, Christmas, that was so bad-ass. You be fine as hell in my eyes."

She giggles. "Thanks, I guess."

"I'm just messing wit ya. Props, girl; that was sick for sure."

Curly jumps in. "Yeah! That, 'Child's play' line, where'd that come from?"

Christi says, "Actually, I heard it from my brother when he was playing one of those old-ass shooter games. In the moment, it just came to me. "

"Well, it was dope."

"Thanks."

Clove chimes in: "How did you come up with all that, girl?"

Christi explains, "For two weeks, I practiced how to beat Sonny at his own game. I couldn't do it. Even if I got down the mountain, it wasn't fast enough. Spark's smoke wall was legit, but I had to beat Sonny's time. Vivian sent a text about surprising Sonny. Would Christmas be special without the surprise of presents? So, I added a few. I decided the only way to beat Sonny was to be a bullet and go straight down the slope."

"So, Vivian helped us? My girl," Rose says. She slams the window and demands, "To the Bridge, baby."

29.

A BITTERSWEET CELEBRATION

WHEN WE GET TO THE Bridge our celebration is over. We enter and Twitch sits alone in the booth. He mocks Sonny sitting with his leg up smoking Mixy's Spliff. He says, "Damn, there's my girl. That was so bad-ass." He sits up and pulls down his old baseball hat. "Screw Sonny. He deserved being faced like that in front of the whole world. Now get over here and let's finish this."

Huddled around the booth, the Brigade plans for the Snow Brawl.

"Alright Clove, what can you tell us about the Cherries?" I ask.

Clove spreads a few pictures along the table showing the size of Sonny's minions for the Snow Brawl.

Shit. They're all the size of Irish.

Clove says, "They may be big, but they're dumb. They've been devouring cinnamon jawbreaker Sweets infused with steroids. The kids can't even go to school without hitting a teacher. We have to be smarter."

Irish pats me on the back and asks, "Jester, what's the plan?"

"Well, it's going to take the whole Irish Brigade."

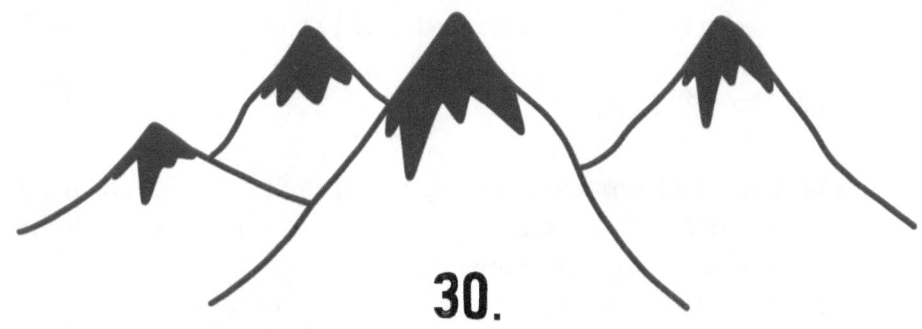

30.

FAMILY TIME

THE NEXT MORNING, I get in the limo and Irish sits with the Brigade. I ask, "Irish, is it cool if we make a pit stop and pick Christi up?'

"For sure."

"Where's Rose?" I ask.

Benny turns on Christi's street, Irish says, "Taking care of her dad."

In all the craziness, I totally forgot about Jimmy.

When we pull up to Christi's house, her entire family is standing on the porch, waving at us like they're posing for a group portrait.

I open the limo door, and Mrs. Daye yells, "Hey Jester!"

Christi darts back, "Mom! Stop it!"

"Love you, honey!" Mr. Daye yells.

"Ah! Dad! You're so embarrassing!"

She turns around and throws her hood up, blowing a piece of disheveled hair off her face and rolling her eyes. She jumps in the limo, I follow, and she sits, giving me a good morning kiss, and says, "Thank god, you guys showed up. I can't get my family off me. Hey, Irish."

He responds with a smile.

She's glowing. I don't want this to end. The limo doesn't seem as dark anymore.

Irish asks, "Why did you need us to pick you up?"

After a heavy breath, she says, "Just didn't want to go into the Hall alone for the first day back, I guess. Still a little weird."

"Really? Why?" I ask.

"Well, not as much the Hall, it's just that our house phone has been booming non-stop from sponsors, reporters, even random fans from across the world. My dad had to unplug the phone and turn off all the cells to let us sleep. I just need some time to breathe."

"Take all the time you want," Irish says. "Ashton is yours now."

As we pull up to Ash High and approach the doors, Christi stalls at the height of the sound.

I hold her.

Reticent, she rests her head on my shoulder like a warming pup and rubs her head.

The doors open and the Hall is rocking as though the party never stopped. The only difference is the Quarters have been blended. Instead of hoods on benches, the entire floor is flooded in Freshmores, Smokes, and Points; even a few Academic kids are sprinkled around, talking about last night's party.

One small Fresh squeals at the sight of Christi and the Hall explodes. It seems like the whole school is there jumping up and down, as pencils, pens, cig sticks, Sweets, and water bottles are showered at her feet. Chirp has built a display of gifts from the valley along the Q1 bench. Christi sits down and the glow on her face makes me shiver.

The crowd is full of wonder and ready to continue the celebration until the doors open again. Like an inverse of Christi's entrance, the crowd dissipates to their Quarters as the Cousins push a bruised and bandaged Vivian in a wheelchair. The scene is uneasy. While the energy is still high, it's cloaked with indifference, confusion, and suspense.

Christi stands and walks in a panic in her direction.

"Oh, my god, Vivian. Are you okay?"

She waves the Cousins away and pushes Vivian towards the Q1 bench. Still damaged but showing signs of recovery, Vivian rests her chin on her chest in shame and tries to speak. Instead she dribbles as she stammers, "I... I..."

"Chirp!" Christi yells. "Please go get some paper towels from the bathroom."

Chirp runs and returns with the towels. Christi wipes both Vivian's mouth and her tears from her cheeks. "It's okay, Viv, take your time."

Vivian raises her chin. The Hall gasps.

"Viv!" Christi shouts.

"It's… it's… I'm sorry," Vivian mumbles.

"No need to apologize." Christi flicks a few fingers towards the Cousins and commands, "Butter, Scotch help her out of the chair. Chirp, please push that stuff off the bench."

Christi whispers into Vivian's ear: "Truth is, I don't even know what I'm doing. And I hate telling Chirp what to do. Could you help me out?"

Vivian raises her head with tears falling and hugs Christi like a soldier seeing a lost comrade return from war.

Choking a bit, Christi jokes, "Okay, okay, but I got to breathe first."

The morning bell rings. Principal Sweeney gives us a half-day to prepare.

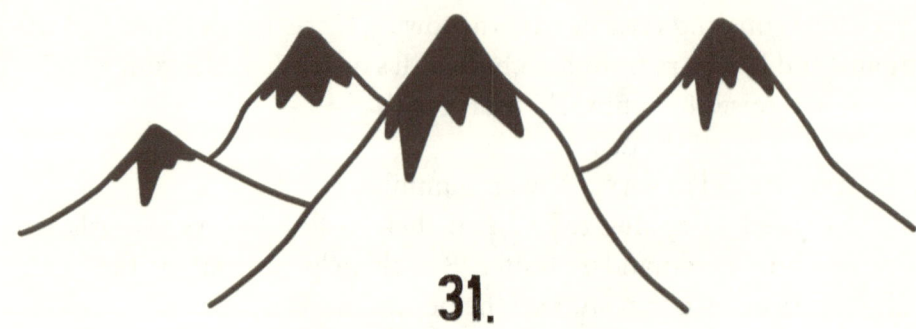

31.

SNOW BRAWL
ON THE PITCH

COUNTLESS HELICOPTERS SOAR overhead televising for the rest of the world the upcoming explosive events. The sun falls over the snow peaks, blending the streaks of purple, orange, blue, and cotton-candy pink. Snowflakes the size of bottle caps swirl through the calm air.

A docked, grass pitch sits alone on the Cherry Ridge side of Powder Lake for the final Snow Brawl match. On one side of Snowdrop Stadium sit the Cherries, stoic and proper in suits and top hats, with the women draped in fur. Opposite are the rowdy fanatics of Ashton puffing smoke and drinking. Grass blanketed in snow, we face Sonny and his Cherries on the pitch, separated by ten yards.

The speakers resonate with the on-field sounds of our preparation. Even our breathing can be heard through field audio transmitters.

Rex and Barry stand on the sideline and begin their transmission.

Rex: "Welcome world to the final competition in Powder Valley between the Ashes of Ashton and The Cherries of Cherry Ridge. The simplistic but most violent competition, The Snow Brawl, will determine the winner of the Powder Match."

Barry: "Ah, the smell of the grass still brings back memories."

Memories of blood and gore.

Rex: "The Snow Brawl can be brutal, even animalistic. Taken loosely from the Japanese Bo-Taoshi, this finale draws the largest television audience by far. Each team can bring up to ten kids, whether or not they've participated in the earlier rounds. A single pole will be dropped from the sky at the center of the pitch. The pole has two flags attached to its peak. The first team to remove their flag from the pole is rewarded a precious thirty seconds to line up a defense.

"In order to win, a team must capture the pole and bring it their side of the field. If a brawler is smashed to the ground and does not get up for 30 seconds, they are removed from the pitch."

The 6:55 siren sounds off. We have five minutes to prepare.

Sonny has chosen nine teammates the size of Irish. I've never seen any of these ringers before.

Irish, Curly, Mars, Shea, Clove, Butter, Scotch, Christi, Twitch (with Mixy's Spliff in mouth) and I face Sonny and his army. Sonny's soldiers hold cinnamon "Jaw Breakers" in their mouths. Our breath plumes burst forward like Clydesdales stomping through giant snow drifts. The night lights blast on us as the sun makes its descent. A slow and thunderous airplane reverberates over our heads. It drops a pole with spear-like points from the night sky.

With an ear-piercing boom, it lands at the center of the pitch. Not a muscle moves.

6:57.

We huddle together. All of sudden, Dooby sneaks in through our huddle with a pouch attached to his collar.

Doobs! Doobs?

Tied to the pouch is a small raveled note from Mixy. "Thanks for everything! Put it on! My parents made it personally for you. Good luck, guys!"

Inside the pouch are small bottles of lotion for each person. We each rub the lotion into our faces and once it seeps into our bloodstream, euphoria and adrenaline take over. We feel no pain. The Snow Brawl is not just a physical battle but chemical warfare.

6:59.

In our huddle, we finalize the plan. I say, "Christi, we need to defend that pole. You have to get that flag. Irish gets Sonny. We get the pole."

The Brigade, hit by the lotion, stares at its enemies.

10 seconds.

    5 seconds.

        3…

            1…

The starter pistol pops.

Christi bolts with Butter and Scotch on her sides. Sonny sends three kids thick as boulders. They charge together like speeding trains.

A beast Cherry lowers his shoulders to head barrel Christi, but sly and quick, she uses the snow to slide past him, curling his left leg, making him fall face first to the ground. The sound of his leg snaps through the stadium. With both knees, she jumps on his back and elbows him until he is immobile.

Butter, leaner and taller, and Scotch, dodge in and out in a spontaneous labyrinth pattern. They meet the other two Cherries and throw elbows and fists to their chins, groins, and chests. The two Cherries scream and the energized excitement turns to silence. The speakers aren't needed, but still blast around the pitch.

Christi scales the pole and grabs the flag. She gives our team some time to surround the pole. We set up a barrier. Sonny sends an all-out blitz and the remaining Cherries lumber in our direction.

We stand our ground as they charge into our line.

Curly, Mars, Clove, Twitch and Irish join hands and form a clothesline. Knuckles crash against cartilage and muscle. The Cherries scream as the fellas pummel them, but they don't quit. One after one, the momentum of each brawl shifts.

The Cherries take over and we counter attack. We may have the lotion, but they have size. They take us down in seconds. It is mayhem. Our barrier is broken; Sonny runs for the pole. Beating bones haunt the air. Christi clings to the pole like a helpless cat. Sonny hurls himself against the pole. Christi is thrown off and crashes to the ground. She and the pole lie parallel to each other, motionless.

Rex: "Looks like the Queen hurt herself!"

Irish jumps with two feet to Sonny's chest and knocks him on his back. He stomps him and throws his left and right elbows at his jaw. He picks Sonny up and body slams him to the ground. Irish then runs to help Christi. He scoops her up to carry her away from the fight. Sonny runs and kicks the back of Irish's knee.

Cheap ass!

Sonny throws his own powerful elbow-blows to Irish's face. Each blast to his nose and jaw echo through the pitch like snapping plastic.

I try to enter the pitch, but I'm stopped by a strong palm to the chest. It's Rose. "Rose? What are you doing?"

Jesus, Rose. What the hell!?

Her eyes are blood-red and she heaves like a devil. Her breath smells from the Sweet she's chewing. She's increased almost twice her size. Thick muscles ripple across her body. A muscular amazon. She growls in a deep voice, "You think I was going to let you fight the Cherries without me? You're my Jester. And every Jester needs its *true* Irish."

Rex: "What am I seeing? An Amazon?"

She sweeps me aside to charge the field. Her black hair flows like a cape. She reaches the pole and lifts it off the ground for the rest of the Irish Brigade to carry, and leaves to take care of Irish. Sonny beats him in fury. Rose kicks Sonny in the back and he sprawls to the ground. She grabs Irish by the hood and flings him backwards near the pole like a doll.

She marches to Sonny and hoists him to his feet. She kneels. Vulnerable, she distracts an enraged, Sonny. He bombards her with left and right fists. The crowds are stunned at the sight of the first female sacrificing herself in the Snow Brawl. The brawlers are stunned as well. The stadium is silent. The pitch is silent. Fighting stops. Her diversion works.

I look to the pole and the fellas huddle around Irish. He only has ten seconds to get up.

I scream, "Irish! Irish! Irish!"

Nothing.

"REGINALD!"

His head jolts up.

Irish pushes himself up, our eyes meet and he sees my fear. He lifts the pole off the ground.

After one last blow to the face, Sonny jams his fist into Rose's side and she falls. He runs for his last stand. Sonny charges as the fellas trudge with the pole. Feet away from the line, Sonny reaches our pole, but Christi, out of nowhere, hook slides his feet, sending him sprawling. We cross the line.

Rex: "Ashton wins!"

An air horn shrieks, signaling the end of the contest.

An astonished hush falls over the stadium. Once reality sets in, the Ashes roar in victory and storm the pitch. A crowd surges around me. I try to find Rose, but like the rest of the Brigade, I'm lifted off my feet and tossed in the air like confetti. A bleeding Irish bulls through the crowd to get to her. Before he reaches her, she has shrunken to her normal size. He wraps an arm around her waist and carries her to the crowd. Despite her injuries, she manages a smile as we are celebrated like victorious gods.

32.

JUBILATION

O N THE RIDE BACK, the celebration is different. It's broken. We won, but the Brigade is hurt. Our faces are smashed plums with blood. Followed by heavy breaths, a few broken coughs and whimpers fill the dead air.

Irish lights a cig stick, but only takes a puff before he hears Rose cough. He places the stick in his cantine. A trickle of blood creeps down her chin. "Rosey, what's wrong?" he asks. "Are you okay?"

Irish removes his hoodie and rips a bloody sleeve of his t-shirt to wipe off Rose's mouth. His arm is purple, which means his body is even worse.

I ask, "What happened out there, Rose?"

Weak, she speaks, "I stole the Sweet from my dad."

"You didn't even know what it did?" Irish asks, pissed at her.

She responds with a look to Christi, "Irish, you told Christi she had to be fearless to beat Sonny. I'm not afraid of the consequences. The Cherries deserve what they got."

Still pissed, Irish stares out the window, shaking his head as we cross the Dam.

Silence. Snow Queen chants vibrate the limo. We approach the Ashton crowd and it separates to leave a path for us to enter. The limo stops; hundreds of Ashton hoodies are laid across the street ahead.

Christi whispers, "I can't... I don't... I don't know what to say."

I stop her. I speak to the crowd for her. "We've been hiding in the shade for years!" I yell.

"We've now shown the entire world the power of Ashton. Pull your hoods back. Raise your glasses, kiss and hug your loved ones. Tonight is a night to rejoice. For the Irish have risen."

The crowd erupts. I raise my hand. "Just one more gift from Christmas, Mixy's family, and Irish and me... to you." I point behind them. Curly and Mars stand with barrels full of new concoctions of Sweets. I pick one up and the wrapper is black with a white bow saying, "The Big Deal Sweet." I look at the effects side of the wrapper and its simply says: marijuana-infused.

Hmmm... The Kombows must have found a way to sneak marijuana plants from the Cherries.

Handful after handful, they toss them to the crowd.

We stay for a bit, shaking hands. Christmas signs a few autographs, and dances with kids from the school.

We pull up to the Bridge, and when the doors open, everybody jumps out except Christi and me. Christi pulls me down.

"What's up?" I ask.

"You think we could use the limo for a little bit?" Christi asks.

"You're the Queen," I tease. "We can do anything."

"You know I don't like being called that when it's just us."

I kiss her hand to apologize. "I know, Sweetie. I just don't know what to do with all this happiness."

Irish leans in and asks, "You comin', man?"

"Nah... I think we're just going to take the limo, if that's cool?"

"For sure."

He shuts the door, slams the top of the limo for Benny to drive, and Christi and I hold each other.

We stop atop the Hill. Benny gives us time alone. I turn on the heat and open the moon roof. With the sky cloudless, the moon beams a soft blue light into the middle of the limo. We turn on the music to a classic R&B station and lie together. I rub her thigh, bruised from the fall. We've kissed countless times before, and a few times fooled around, but this time my mind races as Christi's intensity is awesome, and I don't know what to do with myself. Christi reaches in her purse and pulls out a condom. She climbs on top of my lap, pulls off her top, unstraps her bra, and places my hands on her warm breasts. With my pants about to burst, she unbuckles my belt and unbuttons my top button. She attempts to put the condom on herself, but it snaps and flies against my face. "Oh, I am so sorry," she says. Her embarrassment makes her more alluring for some reason.

"It's fine, ha. Let me see." I say.

I have to stop her to catch my breath. I attempt to push her away and just for a moment, I get out the word "wait," but it's useless as she presses her chest to my face to shut me up. As much I want to continue, I fight the urge, hold her shoulders, and gently, reluctantly, push her away. I catch my breath and she asks, "What? What's wrong?"

"Nothing's wrong. This is awesome. I just want to make sure you're ready for this."

"Aren't you?" she asks.

"Well yeah, I've been thinking about every day, and most nights of my life, especially with you, but…"

"But what?"

"I just want to make sure this is what you really want."

"Dammit, J. Could you just be the man I know you are?"

I grab her by the waist, pull her up, and bring her to the floor of the limo. She pulls down her pants, she takes off mine, and the "bases" are covered in a matter of seconds. The next hour is a blur and a blend of awkward awesomeness.

I'm the luckiest man in the valley.

We head back to the Bridge and music blasts. Mom, Jimmy, and Jameson sit in our booth. Jimmy asks for Seamus to lock the door. Once the door is locked, Seamus heads to the cellar, but Jimmy stops him. "You're finest water, Seamus. I want to remember tonight." Seamus brings a large bottle of cherry-flavored sparkling water. Jimmy raises his glass and begins an Irish Brigade cheer. "To the old and the new, the green and the blue, true Irish we are, forever, near and far."

We lift our glasses and begin to celebrate. Jimmy asks for the table to leave us alone. He begins. "I'm sorry about that scene back at the house. My PTSD spells are getting worse."

"It's okay, Jimmy. Mom's are just as bad."

His left eye waters. He pinches a lone tear and says, "Your dad was a great man."

"I know."

Jimmy looks me in the eyes to make sure I hear.

"I miss your dad more than anything. He was like a brother to me. Your mom a sister. He'd be proud of you, you know."

He looks at Rose and Irish resting in their own booth, holding hands. A smile creases from the right side of his mouth when he looks over at Clove coughing from some weed in Curly's Quarter.

"How's Jameson?" I ask.

He shrugs. "You know, I don't know J. But at least I have her back. I have my family back.

"Rose told me what you two did. None of this would have happened if it weren't for you, J. … Thanks."

He shakes my hand and presents the rest of the Bridge with his other and says, "The best part is *after* all the shit. Now go have some fun. That's an order."

"Thanks, Jimmy."

He and Mom leave.

The rest of the night is a blurred celebration. Ashes dance in the streets like years past. Twitch smokes Mixy's concoction and for the first time in a long time, we get to hang out. My stomach hurts from all the laughter. It's like heaven traded places with hell for the night.

The Bridge is different. Instead of separate booths, everyone intermingles like family. Curly and Mars spit game at the Chicklets. Christi and I join Rose and Irish.

Christi starts.

"So, we did it!"

"That we did!" Irish shouts over the room.

I smack him and say, "Dude, we did it. We have the money. We have the land. We have the trophy. We saved our people."

I look to Rose and she can only shrug in confusion.

Irish lights a cig stick and says, "We still need water."

I say, "Jesus, man, look what we did. Look what *you* did."

"*I* didn't do anything."

Rose starts coughing. Blood drips out. She covers her mouth.

Irish asks, "What's wrong, Rosy?"

"Nothing," Rose says. "Can we go home? I'm not feeling too well."

As I stand, about to tell everyone to leave, Rose pulls me back down in the booth. She points to the center of celebration.

"Don't you dare ruin this, for me. I can walk out," she says defiantly. *Something's wrong.*

Irish walks her out. She stumbles, but makes her way out of the Bridge.

33.

BRUISED ROSE

THE NEXT MORNING, I wake up next to Christi with Mom slamming her fist against the door, screaming. Groggy, I unlock the door and ask, "What's up, Ma?"

In frantic breaths, she says, "It's Rose... she's not... she's not... she's in the hospital."

"What?" My mind snaps fully awake.

"She's in the hospital. The only person she'll talk to is you."

"Me?"

"I don't know! But Jimmy is freaking out and threatening people."

"All right, take care of Christi. I'll call ya in a bit. Love ya, Mom."

While we walk outside, the limo is already running. I get in and the Brigade is in the car with hoods pulled over. Irish is gone. No one speaks. The ride over is painfully quiet.

Once at the hospital, I enter an empty Emergency Room to hear a madman screaming a few halls down. "Jimmy!" I yell.

Jimmy paces back and forth, helpless. I see Jameson and Clove holding each other. Jimmy runs and hugs me with terrified tears.

"Calm down... breathe... what happened?" I ask him.

Jimmy says, "I... I... don't know. All I remember is seeing her cough a few times and Irish carry her out. They won't let me see her.

They won't let me see my baby girl, J. She'll only see you. Help, please! I'll do anything."

I look in his eyes and say, "Breathe. I'll see what's up. Go have a drink in the limo. I'll talk to her."

He says, "Thanks."

I walk in the hospital room and a scrum of doctors and nurses huddle around a bed, where Rose lies with tubes connected all over her body. One doctor turns to me, "Her kidney is lacerated. With surgery and time, she may get better. I'm sorry."

I move close to her bed.

She pulls the oxygen mask off and struggles to speak. "Find, Irish," she says.

"Why? What's going on? My voice cracks. "What happened?" I ask.

She coughs and spits up blood. A nurse dabs her bib with a napkin.

She struggles to pull at my collar and whispers, "Find Irish, now."

It hits me.

Irish is a man that can get things. Shit.

I blast through the doors. Jimmy looks at me. "Go see your daughter," I say.

I rush to the limo where I order Benny: "Irish's house! Now!"

Benny burns through Ashton twisting, turning, drifting, almost crashing all the way up to Irish's cabin. The snow sheets around us. I see Irish through a graveyard of cut-down trees. He's hacking away at a massive tree, drinking a bottle of whiskey.

Why's he drinking?

"Irish! What are you doing, man?"

He pounds the rest of the bottle and takes a massive swing at the trunk. The tree starts to fall. I sprint towards him. He stands firm. I attempt to tackle him, but he slides to the left. I slip and fall down a hill to a nearby flowing creek. The cold water shocks me. I stagger to my feet, shivering and wondering where all the water came from.

I look around. It hits me. Irish hasn't been cutting down trees for money and strength. He's been making a dam.

I hear cracking branches and an eventual boom. I bear crawl to the top and see him almost broken in half. I slide next to him trying to lift the trunk, but it's useless. Blood pours underneath his body. He tries to push himself up, but fails, laughing.

"Jesus, that hurt more than I thought," he says.

He looks around his body and tries to get up.

I mutter, "You fool. What were you thinking?"

"Rose needs my body more than I do."

I look around for a place to grab the trunk and lift, but I'm not strong enough.

"Irish, I can't save you."

"You already have."

He hacks up blood and with shaking hands asks, "J., remember me asking about the future? About after high school?"

"Yeah man. Jesus, who cares?"

He looks at the creek.

"Now you have it. A future."

I consider the creek and understand what he means.

With water comes power.

I see a pond a few yards away. His eyes begin to twitch as reality sets in and his face shows serious pain. He pulls me down. "I died with my mom. I know you'll do what's right. Thanks, brother... for giving me a life."

"No way, dude!" I fish a cell phone from my pocket. "The ambulance will be here soon. Just hold on."

His eyes dim. "Take care of my Rosey. I've left her the best part of me. Love's never died... it just looks a little different these days." His eyes roll back and the light in them is gone. I feel him grow cold. I hear myself whimper, begging him not to leave me, but it's useless. My Irish is dead. My brother is gone.

34.

AN IRISH GRAVE

THE NEXT SIX WEEKS are hellish, especially for Rose. Doctors repaired one kidney, but both kidneys are weak, damaged by the Sweets she took. Once the doctors let her out, her first instinct is to visit Irish's grave. I pick her up in my mom's truck and we head to his cabin.

We are joined by the Irish Brigade. Twitch holds the polar bear in his left arm and a single tear trickles down his cheek. He finishes carving Irish's gravestone with a quote from James Joyce: "Absence, the highest form of presence."

Curly and Mars empty Irish's water cantine on the stone, watching it trickle down, down, down. We sit on Irish's sacrificial log. Christmas rests on my arm, Rose's head is on my shoulder. She flicks Irish's lighter and brushes her side. She says, "I will always have a part of him."

"I know. He was a hell of man from the day I met him," I say.

"What are we going to do now?" Christi asks.

"Find another Irish, I guess," I say.

Rose rubs her belly. After taking a sip of water, she says, "Well, we may not have to wait very long."

ACKNOWLEDGMENTS

I WOULD NOT HAVE COMPLETED this novel if it weren't for the continued support from my family. I love you guys. Thank you Dad, Mom, Meghan, and Derek. Also, many thanks to my extended family in Rochester, New York, for taking the time to read and provide feedback.

I want to show my appreciation for those that believed in my written word before the creation of *Irish Town*. I was a relentless writing teacher when I taught elementary school, and I want to say to all of my students: "Play it cool, keep it real, and you'll be a big deal." Specifically, I want to thank the Spence family and the McGuire family for their support.

Many thanks go to the professors and mentors of Regis University. Your tutelage and expertise helped build a small idea into a novel. Mario Acevedo, Traci Jones, David Hicks, and Denise Vega, thank you. I want to acknowledge Hugh Cook for editing Irish Town. Your skills for line editing are unmatched. I learned a lot during my work with Hugh. Irish Town would not exist if it weren't for his work.

Further thanks go to my friends: Adam Markert, Andrew Mumaugh, Sean Riley, Brian Ireland, Mitch Ludwigson, Lance Renes, Ally Levise, Kristen Sheble, Michaela McKenna, Tim Hopkins, Bryce Gartner, Graham Colegrove, Tyler, and Aspen Spratt.

Thank you to the Medical Center of Aurora for your counseling. My passion for writing sprouted when we were working together.

ACKNOWLEDGMENTS

I want to thank Louise Zimmerman, Matt Jarvis, Cheyenne Edmunson, and Sam Mingle for your support.

Lastly, I want to acknowledge you the reader. Thank you for taking the time to read my story and I hope you enjoy!

ABOUT THE AUTHOR

Photo by Cassandra Vagher

Matt is a native of Colorado growing up in Englewood, south of Denver.

After graduating from the University of Northern Colorado, he became a fifth grade teacher specializing in writing.

After seven years of teaching Matt decided to pursue his own writing career and entered the Master of Fine Arts in Creative Writing program at Regis University where he wrote his premier novel *Irish Town*.

"I wanted to write a book that everyone would enjoy with engaging and relatable characters. Mostly, I wanted my readers to have fun."

He is currently working on two additional writing projects as well as developing his writing consulting business MARSMEN Ltd.